Annie O'Neil spent most of her childhood with her leg draped over the family rocking chair and a book in her hand. Novels, baking, and writing too much teenage angst poetry ate up most of her youth. Now Annie splits her time between corralling her husband into helping her with their cows, baking, reading, barrel racing (not really!) and spending some very happy hours at her computer, writing.

A RETURN, A REUNION, A WEDDING

ANNIE O'NEIL

MILLS & BOON

First published in Great Britain 2019
by Mills & Boon, an imprint of HarperCollins*Publishers*
1 London Bridge Street, London, SE1 9GF

Large Print edition 2020

© 2019 Annie O'Neil

ISBN: 978-0-263-08540-2

FLINTSHIRE SIR Y FFLINT		
C29 0000 1223 691		:ertified ;ement. For uk/green.
ULV	£16.99	4YY

This book goes, without reservation, to my new editor Sheila. I asked her to help make me a better writer and she took me at my word. Hopefully you'll enjoy the results! May it be the first in a long list of HEAs we craft together xo

CHAPTER ONE

JAYNE SHOULD HAVE been getting fist-bumps right now. High-fives. A group hug. Not watching a mass exodus from her operating theatre.

What on earth was going on?

She pulled off her surgical gown, gave her face a quick scrub, and deposited it into the laundry bin.

'All right there, Dr Sinclair?'

The hospital's favourite surgical nurse, Sana, didn't body-block her, exactly, but... Why was the rest of the surgical team high-tailing it out of there?

Peculiar.

Maybe they all had hot dates. Or on-call rooms to collapse in.

Ten hours of heart transplant surgery was tiring. For most people, anyway. Sana looked as energetic as ever. Maybe it was the dancing unicorns on her scrubs.

Sana fixed Jayne with her bright smile.

'Somebody's frown is upside down. And we don't do that here at the London Merryweather Children's Hospital. Not after a successful surgery.'

'I'm not frowning.' Jayne fought to smooth the furrow between her eyes.

Okay, fine. The surgery had been tough… but it wasn't as if she wanted to *talk* about it.

'The Jayne Sinclair I know doesn't frown. So…' Sana popped her hands on to her hips. 'Are you going to explain to me what's broken your smiley face or am I going to have to start pulling teeth?'

Jayne tried to look away and couldn't.

Oh, crumbs. So this was *The Sana Look.*

Five years at the Merryweather and she'd never once seen it. If the rumour mill was anything to go by it was pointless to resist.

The Sana Look, as it was known in hospital parlance, was something to actively avoid. It was responsible for all sorts of madness. The Head of Paediatric Surgery had buckled under its strength, finally fulfilling a lifelong dream to climb Mount Kilimanjaro. Registrars fled to cosy cottages in Devon to tackle long-neglected 'To Read' piles. Nurses skipped around theme parks in Florida. Even the aptly named Dr Stayer, who was rumoured never to have once taken a day of holiday in his thirty years of practice, had handed in his notice and was learning how to surf in Bali at this very moment.

No one was immune.

When Sana gave *The Look*, the HR department listened. As did the hospital's Chief Executive. It was that powerful. It meant one thing and one thing only: *someone needed to take a holiday.*

Jayne shuddered. Already she could see her six weeks of unused holiday waiting to pounce and attack.

Nooo!

She didn't do breaks. Or downtime. She certainly didn't casually hand in holiday requests. She did surgery. And extra shifts. And proactively offered a helping hand wherever she could in the hospital so that she could become the best paediatric cardiologist possible. This was her happy place. Here she could fix things. Out there she… Well, she and London had never exactly bonded.

She swept her hands across her face and turned her frown into a smile. 'Nothing to worry about on this front, Sana. See?' She struck a jaunty pose. 'Happy face!'

Sana gave her one of those slow head-to-toe scans that said, *Girlfriend...try telling that to the judge.*

Jayne shifted uncomfortably.

'You did a great job...' Sana said, in a way that had a big fat 'but' lying in wait.

'Always a good day when I can fix a heart.' *If only she could fix her own.*

Sana arched an eyebrow as if she'd heard the silent plea.

It had been one tear. Just the one! A tear that had been shed *well* after the critical part of the surgery had been finished. Jayne's hands had been clear of the patient. The other surgeons had been closing under her supervision. Nothing for Sana to get all *Looky* over.

Sana crossed her arms over her chest and started humming. She was patient. More than that... She was well-versed in cocky young surgeons lying about their feelings after particularly tough surgeries.

If only she knew just how tough this one had been...

Jayne's patient—a gorgeous, bright and very funny fourteen-year-old called Stella—had been on a mechanical heart for five months now. An epic stretch of time for anyone to endure that level of heart failure, let alone a kid. Her family was exhausted from putting on a brave face. Not to mention bearing the weight of constant fear that came with the simple fact that one day Stella's body simply might not be able to handle being put through the mill any more.

When a donor heart had become available early that morning Jayne and her team had been elated. They'd pulled in every favour in the book to get it to London and into the patient's chest, where it was now beating away all on its own.

It should have been a landmark moment. For Stella, obviously. But for Jayne, too.

She'd spent over ten years of her life training, studying, and fine-tuning herself to become a paediatric cardiologist—just as her twin sister Jules had imagined *she* would be one day.

Her heart seized so hard and tight she could hardly breathe. She needed to get out of here.

Her eyes darted to the doors of the operating theatre and once again Sana's brown eyes appeared in front of her. *Looking.*

This wasn't how she'd pictured this moment. Completing a full heart transplant surgery was meant to have been an epically happy day for her. The day that she finally fulfilled her sister's dream.

As she shrank under Sana's unblinking gaze she felt her blood begin to chill in her veins. Maybe fulfilling someone else's destiny didn't work that way.

If she were Jules she'd be leading a parade to the pub right now. Buying the first round. Toasting her team of fellow surgeons, nurses, nephrologists, immunologists and all the other medical professionals who'd helped make this critical surgery a reality. Daring everyone to join her in a charity skydive.

Not being stared down by Sana.

Okay, fine! Blubbing over a patient wasn't the done thing in transplant surgery. Which was why there were rules in place. And yet the one rule...the *only* rule...of her operating theatre when she was about to place one person's vital organ into another person? Oh, *that* rule had been well and truly broken.

No. Unnecessary. Details.

A good heart was a good heart. Origin stories weren't necessary. They made her emotional. There wasn't a person on earth who was served well by an emotional surgeon.

Committed? Passionate? Intense?

Absolutely. Jayne admitted to all those things. Proudly.

Sure, it was important to know *some* things about donor organs. Suitability. Viability. Accessibility. Jayne always checked the facts. She also ran a slew of tests. Bloods, X-rays, tomography, MRIs, ultrasounds. Not to mention the coronary angiography and the cardiac catheterisation. She'd done each and every one of them with the exacting scientific precision they had required. And then asked for the flow of information to stop there.

One of the junior surgeons on her team simply hadn't got it. Just as she'd lifted the heart into her hands he'd blurted out the origin story of the donor.

That was when the first sting of tears had hit.

She'd crushed them, of course.

But it had been tough.

The donor heart had come with strings attached. Strings that went all the way back to the worst day in Jayne's life. The heart she had successfully transplanted into Stella had belonged to a young woman who'd been out for a bicycle ride on a country lane.

Just like Jules. Jayne's twin.

Neither young woman had returned home. Neither had heard their sister calling frantically for the car to stop. Neither one had lived to fulfil their destinies. Because both of them had been declared brain-dead at the scene. So if Jayne's smile wasn't hitting her eyes she had a damn good reason why.

She heard a page on the intercom and made a dash for the door. 'Pretty sure that's Stella's room.'

Sana started laughing and body-blocked her. 'Easy there, tiger. That was for Dr Lewis. It's his wife.'

'How do you even *know* that?' She'd not heard a single word of the page.

Sana's face softened with one of those warm, all-knowing smiles of hers. 'She always rings around now, to find out whether or not she should put his supper on.'

'Ah.'

A twist of envy squeezed the air out of her chest. She could have had that too. Someone who loved her enough to make her supper… cared enough not to burn it…cared if she came home at all…

An image of Sam popped into her head and swiftly she swept it away. No point in swan-diving into ancient history. Even so, she'd bet *he* wouldn't be fazed by Sana's *Look*. He'd shoot her one of those crooked smiles of his. Give her a wink, a hug, and promise they'd sit and talk all she wanted over a cup of tea and a scone down by the river.

He was one of those men who made time for everyone and the expression on his face when she'd handed him back his ring...

Sana gave Jayne's arm a gentle squeeze. 'Go home. Take a bath. Do whatever you do to unwind. Then take some *real* time off. You've dedicated yourself to Stella for months. This is when you let the rest of the team look after her.'

Jayne bristled. 'No way. Until her body accepts that heart I'm staying.'

The Look reared up, strong and powerful. 'When's the last time you took a holiday? And I'm not talking about the two days a year you take off to throw some Christmas presents at your parents, either.'

Ouch.

'You cried. In surgery.' Sana rolled her finger. 'And the reason why was...?'

Jayne tried to turn away, but it was as if Sana's eyes were pouring invisible cement into her trainers. Lemon juice into her seven-years-old wounds.

Was this what *The Sana Look* did? Brought things to the surface that you'd tried for years to hide?

Sana blinked. Deliberately.

The tiniest hint of perspiration broke out on Jayne's forehead.

Suddenly Jayne was beginning to see the advantage of taking a break. A chance to regroup. Get her emotions back under control. She could go to a boot camp. Or a Mastering Your Inner Ninja week.

The flash of another option sent a complication of emotions pouring through her heart. Maybe she could just...*go home*?

Sana had a point. Everyone's life needed balance, and her life was one hundred per cent devotion to her job. She had no life outside the hospital. She'd tried clubbing, rock-climbing, wild city breaks in Europe's party places, and yet, years later it turned out partying till she dropped, terrifying herself with adrenaline-laced activities and fixing someone else's heart, was never, ever going to bring her sister back.

Which meant...maybe going home to heal some wounds might be a good thing.

Oh. My. Word. What was *happening* to her?

It was *The Look*. No doubt about it.

Sana put her hands on Jayne's shoulders, forcing her to meet her eyes.

'Jayne.' Sana's voice was kind—loving, even. 'You need some time off. What about your parents? They're out near Oxford somewhere, aren't they? Surely they'd love a visit from their surgeon daughter?'

Jayne shook herself free of Sana's hands. Her relationship with her parents had altered irrevocably the day Jules had died. She knew they loved her, but Jules had been one of those rare souls who'd taken people's breath away for all the right reasons. Beautiful, vivacious, crazy, smart...

Risk-taker. Unsettled. Adrenaline junkie.

All the things Jayne wasn't.

'My parents tend to go away in the summer.'

It was Scotland this year. Was it the Outer Hebrides? Somewhere remote, she knew. The fewer cars the better. She had the address in her phone, but the remit was always the same. No cars. Her mother, who'd once shone with a bright passion for life, had been all but literally wrapped in cotton wool ever since the accident.

'Friends, then?' Sana persisted. 'Surely you've

got someone back in Whitticombe who'd love to see you?'

'Not really,' she lied.

Her bestie, Maggie, would put her up in a heartbeat.

As if Sana's inquisition was wringing the truth out of her, she silently admitted there were two very simple reasons she hated going home.

One: she couldn't think of Whitticombe without thinking of her sister's death. A death that never would have happened if she hadn't asked Jules to come home that day to celebrate her engagement. Which led to reason number two. The only thing more painful than helplessly watching the life slip away from her sister had been handing her engagement ring back to Sam.

Urgh!

Sana's suggestion was impossible. Six whole weeks of avoiding The Romance That Might Have Been? The Marriage She'd Always Wanted? The Life She Could Have Had?

Impossible.

She'd missed that boat a long time ago—had practically thrown him the oars. Besides, if Maggie's newsy emails were anything to go by there'd been a whole lot of water under Sam's bridge over the last few years. A marriage. A divorce. His mother's death.

And yet here she was, still stuck on *That Day*...

If she shut her eyes she could see it all in fine detail. It had been sunny. Tourists had been beginning to flood into town to enjoy the iconic sandstone cottages and, of course, the beautiful stone-lined river that lazily wound its way through the heart of the village. It had been early June, as it was now. The usual riot of flowers had been in bloom.

She'd had a shiny new diamond solitaire on her finger.

Jayne had come home from med school to see Sam and he had proposed. Of course she'd said yes. He was the love of her life. Had been since the first perfect kiss they'd shared the day she'd turned sixteen.

Jules had dropped everything and raced home from London. The family's golden girl. They'd all adored her. As usual, she hadn't wanted to settle for anything simple like a toast to celebrate. Jayne had suggested they ride their old bicycles down the lane and on to the pub they'd visited when they were in pigtails. Only this time they'd order a glass of fizz instead of the squash they'd used to ask for.

Jules had been pulling out their bicycles as soon as the suggestion was out there.

Their father had thrown them a distracted wave from his easel—another landscape. Their mother had laughed from her sculpting table and, before waving them off, had done what she'd always done—kissed them each on the cheek, then told them to be safe.

Then she'd thrown in an extra warning to Jayne, as though they were still kids rather than grown women, 'Keep an eye on your sister. You know what she's like.'

Stop at the end of the lane. Check for traffic a hundred times. Proceed to pub. That was the procedure.

Only this time Jules hadn't followed it. She'd taken off at high speed and turned it into a race.

Three hours later…after the ambulance had gone and neighbours had flooded the house to make her parents cup after cup of sweet, milky tea… Jayne had slipped the sparkling ring on and off her finger.

A few months later she'd taken it off for good.

She'd changed in those months. No longer had she been the carefree, optimistic girl Sam had asked to marry him. In her place had come someone more steely-eyed, driven, determined to fulfil the dreams her sister never would.

Jules had always been a bit mad. Her interests wide and varied. But the one thing—the *only* thing—that had captured Jules' high-octane energy had been her desire to perform a paediatric heart transplant.

As the days and then months of grief had built and festered after her death, Jayne had felt every bit as helpless as she had performing CPR on her sister, waiting for help to arrive. Her failure to overcome her sister's catastrophic injuries had set something alight in her that had steered her away from the life she'd planned. A fierce, intense need to make amends for causing her sister's death. To live the life her sister wouldn't. Perform the surgeries her sister wouldn't. Save the lives her sister wouldn't.

She had done that today. Fulfilled her dream. It was meant to have drawn a line in the sand. Loosened the reins on the strict, driven intensity with which she had pursued this goal. Instead it had only proved what she had feared all along—that she hadn't moved on at all.

'Dr Sinclair.' Sana's voice forced her back into the operating theatre. 'If you don't take care of this…' she pointed at Jayne's heart '…you aren't going to be able to look after your patients with *this*.' She pointed at Jayne's head.

Jayne shifted from one hip to the other, then pretended her phone had buzzed.

'Dr Sinclair at your service!' Jayne gave Sana a cheeky wink and mouthed *Sorry*, pointing at the phone. 'Yes! Absolutely. No. No… Nothing on my schedule. I have all the time in the world.'

Sana rolled her eyes.

A code red sounded. Their eyes clashed. They both knew whose room it belonged to. They both knew exactly what it meant.

Three days later, when Jayne heard her own hollow voice call the time of death at the end of Stella's bed, she looked straight into Sana's eyes. She saw everything she needed to know.

It was time to go home.

Sana was right. She had to heal her heart before she could care for any more patients. They deserved her absolute focus, and Stella's death had thrown her right back to the starting line of a race she'd thought she'd finally finished.

Trying to outrun her past was impossible. She

almost laughed as she thought of the advice she regularly gave her own patients.

If you ignore the problem it will only get worse. If you face it head-on you have a chance to live the rest of your life with a few scars. Scars that will make you stronger.

Sam read the final page of the report, then put it on his desk. He turned and looked at his patient. 'So, if I'm reading this right, it's bedrest for the next couple of months, then…eh, Mags?'

'Madness! I can't do that,' his patient wailed. 'There are the children, first of all. Connor's got all sorts of things on, and Cailey's set to have her first ever sports day. The teashop has Dolly, of course, but that place needs my cakebaking skills. Then there's the village fete. I'm on the committee. Obvs.'

Sam smiled. Maggie was on *all* the committees.

'And then there's the fundraiser for the automatic external defibrillator that the village desperately needs. The art fair that I haven't even *begun* to—'

'Whoa! Slow down. What's most important here, Mags? You and the babies. The ones in there.' He pointed at her generously arced tummy. 'Everything else we'll get it sorted, all right?'

Tears pooled in Maggie's eyes as she pressed her fingers to her mouth and nodded.

It was at moments like these that Sam Crenshaw understood exactly why some GPs preferred to start their practices in villages where they *hadn't* known their patients since they were toddlers. Delivering bad news to someone he used to make mud pies with wasn't easy.

Maggie had been to the maternity and children's hospital just outside of Oxford earlier in the day, and had come to him in tears with a sheaf of paperwork detailing just how complicated her pregnancy had become. She'd also told him she'd come up with a solution, but they hadn't quite got to that part yet. Sometimes a patient needed to vent before they could listen…so for now he'd listen. And dole out tissues.

Wiping away a friend's tears was hard…and yet it was precisely why he'd wanted to be a general practitioner right here in Whitticombe. Just like his grandfather.

Their shared love of medicine wasn't genetic. He'd been adopted. Too early to have remembered otherwise but even so the generosity of the Crenshaws, bringing a stranger's child into their already full home, lived in his heart like a beacon. Their credo was to treat people as you wanted to be treated. Lovingly and honestly. That way you never had to hide anything. He liked that.

His family's honesty, openness and love were his foundation. The reason why he'd decided to pursue medicine in the very building where his grandfather had worked for the last forty-odd years. The very building his grandfather refused to retire from!

The bright-eyed rascal loved it. Said he'd have to be dragged from the building rather than retire. Sam was the last person to suggest otherwise. His grandfather was still a highly valued member of the community, and even though Sam had been a GP here for three years now some people still thought of him as the little boy in shorts who'd used to refill the boxes of cotton buds and tongue depressors.

All of which culminated in moments like this. If a person felt vulnerable they should have someone they trusted to come to. If they were frightened or scared? Same thing. And if they were going to hear some very bad news it should come from someone who knew them.

Which was why now he wheeled his chair over to Maggie, took her hands in his and looked her straight in the eye. 'Maggie. I know you're Wonder Woman, but you cannot do this alone. Pre-eclampsia is serious. You need someone who *knows* you to help out. With your parents in Australia, I'll do what I can. We can set up a rota to help with the kids. I can make some calls about your committees—'

His very pregnant patient cut him off with a roll of her eyes. 'You think I haven't thought of all that? I've got it covered. Someone's coming to stay. She's just...' She picked up her phone and gave it a couple of swipes with her finger. 'She should be here any minute. I was hoping you might be able to talk her through everything. With Nate gone and all—'

Maggie's voice hitched and she only just managed to stem another sob. Sam's heart ached for her. Her day had been riddled with bad news. Pre-eclampsia. Danger of premature birth for her twins. Enforced bedrest. And all of this with her Air Force pilot husband stuck in the Middle East until the twins were due. Not to mention taking care of their two little ones.

He hoped this friend of hers had stamina. He could already tell that Maggie was going to run whoever it was ragged.

He went to the supplies cupboard to get a fresh box of tissues and gave himself a stern look in the mirror as he passed. He should carve out more time for Maggie. He was meant to be going for a casual drink with his receptionist's niece tonight. His divorce had gone through over a year ago, so technically it was time to move on. Old news. Today's fish and chip paper, as his grandad would say.

His mum's death earlier in the year had really kicked him in the teeth. Cancer wasn't kind to anyone, and the only blessing that had come from it was that his mother was no longer suffering.

'So who's this friend, then? Why don't you tell me about her? It is a she, right?'

'Yup. Yes.' Maggie suddenly refused to meet his eye. 'She's female all right. Um…'

A quiet tapping sounded at his door. Maggie sat as bolt upright as a woman pregnant with twins could.

'That might be her now.'

Sam crossed the office, opened the door—and there, looking every bit as perfect as she had the day she'd handed him back his diamond solitaire, stood Jayne Sinclair.

She gave a shy little waist-height wave and then, as if they'd rehearsed it, she and Maggie said in tandem, 'Surprise!'

CHAPTER TWO

IF ONE OF Sam's patients had called in with the same physiological responses to a surprise he would have rung an ambulance. Immediately.

Heart slamming against his ribcage. Pulse hitting the red zone. Blood pumping to all the wrong places.

Great. In a little less than the blink of an eye Sam's well-worked theory that the next time he saw Jayne Sinclair it wouldn't so much as register on his heart monitor was blowing up in his face.

He slammed on a mental emergency brake and pulled a sharp U-turn.

Jayne had caught him unawares, that was all. The collapse of their relationship wasn't the only hurdle he'd overcome. He had a marriage, a divorce and his mother's death under his belt now. Making peace with his mountains of emotional baggage had been tough, but he'd done it. Maybe he had a few more grey hairs than he would have thought average for a thirty-one-year-old, but, *that which does not kill us…*

Jayne had had to tackle her own set of emotional hurdles, but time hadn't touched her Snow White aesthetic. Glossy black hair. Bright blue eyes. An English rose complexion that was looking slightly pale considering it was early summer. The Jayne he'd known would have had the kiss of the sun and a smattering of freckles appearing on her nose about this time of year. Twenty-three at the last count.

He forced himself to update his memory banks.

She wasn't the woman he knew any more. That Jayne had all but disappeared the day her sister had been killed.

The 'new' Jayne only came at Christmas. She spent an hour at the pub. No more, often less. Years back they had chatted. Awkwardly. How else could a man exchange Yuletide greetings with the girl he'd thought he'd marry? It wasn't as if he'd asked for the ring back.

At the time—over seven years ago now—he'd actually suggested she keep it. Think about it. Consider the consequences of giving up everything they'd dreamed of. He knew she'd been grieving. Trying to wrap her head round her sister's senseless death. But in the end he'd run out of suggestions. Realised with a cold, numbing clarity that she'd chosen a new path. One that didn't involve him.

As the years had passed their strangulated chit-chat had become a wave. Then a nod. Three years ago, when he'd met and married Marie, it had dissolved into nothing at all. Last Christmas he'd stayed at home because his mum had been so ill. He hadn't let himself consider the option that seeing Jayne so soon after his divorce might reopen wounds he wasn't ready to examine.

Jayne's smile was as unnatural as his own felt. 'Hey, Sam. I hope it's all right that Maggie invited me along?'

As Jayne and Maggie exchanged a quick glance he flexed his hands, willing them not to curl into themselves. He wasn't this guy. Tense. Edgy. Protectively defending his decision to live the life he'd—*they'd*—always dreamed of having.

The life his wife had left behind.

The last three years of his life flashed past in an instant. He'd thought he and Marie were happy. They'd enjoyed a year-long courtship when he'd finished med school. A classic country wedding. A solid year of marriage. The next year hadn't been quite as rosy, but he'd thought he'd made it clear to her that he'd be busy. Extremely busy. The house to build... The medical practice to haul into the twenty-first century... His mother's cancer in full attack mode.

Sure, he'd been vaguely aware of hairline fissures in their relationship, but when Marie had told him she wanted out it had shocked him. She'd said getting married so soon had been a mistake. She'd laid out the truth as she'd seen it.

Sam's priorities were the surgery, refurbishing the old barn and his family. She didn't feel she factored anywhere on that list, and for that reason she wanted to cut her losses before the wounds ran too deep. She'd told him this as she'd served him with divorce papers.

He'd had a card from her after his mother had died, and from the sounds of things she'd already found her special someone.

The fact that he was genuinely happy for her spoke volumes. Nothing like an ounce of truth landing like a ton of bricks in your gut. Which all circled back to the here and now, and the fact that Jayne Sinclair was still registering on his personal Richter scale just like she shouldn't.

He scrubbed the back of his neck and pasted on what he hoped was a passable smile. His focus should be on Maggie, not his debacle of a love-life.

'Come on in.'

He ushered Jayne in, showed her to a chair, accidentally inhaling as that all too familiar scent of sweet peas and nutmeg swept round his heart and squeezed a beat out of it. The way it always had.

The Jayne Sinclair Effect.

How could he have forgotten about that?

You didn't. You put it in a box and hoped it would never get opened again.

'Ta-da!' Maggie waggled jazz hands. 'Here's my friend!'

Jayne put out her hands and heaved her friend up for a hug. Maggie's head just about reached Jayne's chin. Jayne's eyes met and locked with Sam's. A familiar energy that he hadn't felt in years shunted through him. The type of energy that came from being with the person who made him feel whole again.

'You look good,' she muttered above Maggie's pile of auburn curls.

She did too. Different. But good. She was all woman now. As if she'd finally grown in to all five feet nine inches of herself. Still slender. Still with a quirky dress sense that spoke of a woman whose life revolved around a children's hospital. She wore an A-line skirt embroidered with polka dots. A well-worn T-shirt with a unicorn on it. Flip-flops with red satin roses stitched across the straps.

Her black hair was still long. She had a chunky fringe now. The rest of her hair was pulled back into the requisite 'doctor's pony-tail'. A brush or two of mascara framed those kaleidoscope blue eyes of hers. Ocean-blue one minute. Dark as the midnight sky the next. Nothing on her lips apart from a swoosh of gloss. They didn't need anything else.

Except, perhaps, for him to find out if her gloss still tasted of vanilla and mint.

He smashed the thought into submission.

That type of impulse was meant to have died a long time ago. Right about the moment she'd handed his ring back to him.

Jayne blinked and hitched her nose against an obvious sting of emotion. When she opened her eyes again they held tight with his.

Oh, hell.

What he wouldn't give to be able to read all

the secrets she held in those jewel-like eyes of hers.

They'd used to light up when they were planning their wedding. Dreaming of finally refurbishing the old barn. Talking about Jayne's plan to specialise in paediatrics. Sam in geriatrics. They'd used to light up when she saw him come round a corner.

Her sister's death had knocked the light out of her eyes. Even so, he'd refused to believe her when she'd said she didn't love him any more. She'd been through a trauma. She was bound to be different for a while.

Jayne had loved Jules as he loved his own family. Fiercely. Protectively. There was no fighting with a ghost. He got that. He'd thought he could wait it out. Be there for her. But she'd refused his support, again and again. Months had gone by before he'd finally seen the change of heart she'd said she felt. The change that had seen her handing him back his ring for good.

That was the day her eyes had lit up again. Glazed with tears, sure, but he'd felt the flare of life return to her as acutely as he would have felt a lightning strike. And it hadn't been him who had put it there. Holding the ring between them, she'd told him she'd changed disciplines.

She wanted to be a paediatric cardiologist. She didn't want to move back to Whitticombe. She'd taken over Jules's flat in London. She'd told him it was time for him to find someone else to run the surgery with.

That had been the blow that had struck the deepest. She had always known more than anyone how much he valued his family and how important running his grandfather's surgery was to him. His family was his adoptive family—they'd never made any secret of it—but he'd never felt anything less than family. When he'd finally been old enough to register that his future might have been completely different—alone in an orphanage—he'd vowed to stick with them as loyally and as lovingly as they'd stuck with him as they'd brought him up. With all of his heart.

It was then that he'd known he had no choice but to walk away from Jayne and get on with his own life. It had broken his heart to do it, but doing anything else would have been living a lie.

Their intense eye contact broke as Maggie pulled back from the hug and hooked her arm round Jayne's waist so that the pair of them were facing Sam.

'Can you believe it? Jayne rang a few days ago and said she had some time off. So I was all *You've got to come back to the village! Nate's away. We've got the cricket tournament on. And the fete. And the art show.* She was supposed to come tomorrow, but when I rang her from the hospital this morning, to tell her about the pre-eclampsia diagnosis, she dropped everything and came straight away.'

Wow. That got his attention. Jayne didn't drop *anything* to leave the hospital. He dipped his head so he could look into her eyes again. See if he'd missed anything.

As his eyes met hers she looked away and said, 'I have a lot of accrued holiday HR were threatening to give away, so...' She gave a half-shrug and a smile that didn't quite meet her eyes.

Something was off here. Had something gone wrong at the hospital? In her private life? Whatever it was, his gut told him she wasn't here for a bit of R&R. She'd come back to Whitticombe because she *needed* to.

She'd been back before. There were the annual Christmas trips, and he had seen her at his mum's funeral in January. Right at the back of the church, flanked by her parents. He hadn't been surprised when she'd disappeared before the wake, even though he knew as well as she did that his parents had all but considered Jayne part of the family. More so, he was beginning to realise with hindsight, than they ever had Marie.

Anyway... She'd made the gesture. It had been noted.

He forced his thoughts back into their cupboard and slammed the door shut. His complicated past with Jayne wasn't the priority in this scenario. Maggie was.

Maggie who was now talking and laughing as if years of history *wasn't* humming like electricity between her two childhood friends.

'I just can't believe you had holiday *exactly* when I needed you. It's like *kismet*!'

She threw a smirk at Sam, as if he'd spent the past half-hour pooh-poohing her choice rather than being blindsided by his own past.

He felt Jane's eyes on him, met them and held her gaze. *Kismet.* That had been 'their' word.

They'd known each other from school, of course, but they had been busy being kids and, as a twin, Jayne had been pretty inseparable from Jules. The magical 'click' had come when their secondary school teacher had decided to throw out the alphabetical seating plan and change things around. They'd shared a table from that day on. Along with a whole lot of other things.

As he dragged himself along memory lane he could hear Maggie saying something about the cricket tournament. He only managed to tune back in when Jayne mock-admonished Maggie.

'We are doing no such thing, young woman! You're meant to be resting.'

'What are you talking about?' he asked.

They both looked at him as if he'd just missed a large gorilla walking through the room in a tutu.

Jayne put on a gently disapproving face. 'This minx here thinks we should take the kids to the cricket tournament tonight for their supper. Ridiculous, right?'

'Uh…not if we want to eat properly,' Maggie said, as if it were obvious.

She had a point. For all her plus points, Jayne was *not* a cook.

Sam and Maggie looked at Jayne as one.

Her cheeks pinked up. 'What?'

'Well, let's see… How I can put this gently?' Maggie teased. 'I can barely reach the counter and I'm meant to be on bedrest anyway.' She feigned fanning herself like a French countess. 'And, as I remember, your cooking skills are about as good as your ability to stick around in Whitticombe.'

'Ouch, woman! Kick a girl when she's down!'

Jayne poked Maggie in the arm, then threw a quick look in Sam's direction. One long enough for him to see the comment had hit its mark. A protectiveness he hadn't realised he still possessed flared in him. What did that mean? 'Kick a girl when she's down'?

Maggie realised she'd gone too far and started apologising, blaming her hormones, blaming Nate for being gone, blaming life for making her pre-eclampsic at her busiest time of year.

Speaking over her apologies, Jayne was trying to accept the blame herself. She was being too sensitive. She knew Maggie was teasing. It had obviously been a joke. She was here. Maggie could rely on her. Please, please, *please* don't worry.

'Maggie's right, Jayne. About supper,' Sam intervened, before everyone's blood pressure went in the wrong direction. 'The cricket club is putting on a proper barbecue tonight and it would be a shame to miss it. The kids will love it. There's going to be a minis' match to kick things off. Sausages. Burgers. I think there are even marshmallows.'

He resisted the temptation to reach out as he would have in the old days and put a reassuring hand on Jayne's shoulder.

'You've had a long drive, no doubt. And Maggie's *definitely* supposed to be taking it easy. Amongst others, my sisters are cooking. I heard one of them mention potato salad at the coffee shop this morning.'

He nudged this comment in Jayne's direction. His sisters made Jayne's favourite potato salad. Unless that had changed, too.

'Sounds good,' she conceded with a grateful smile. But that playful look in her eyes was missing. And then it hit him. It hadn't been there since she'd walked into the room.

Sure, there was the whole awkward 'running into your ex' thing, but they'd seen each other before since they'd split up, at the pub over Christmas, and had just about hit the casual acquaintance kind of comfort level. A quick *Hi, you look well. So do you. Well…happy Christmas, then!* and off they'd go and live their lives for another year.

He narrowed his eyes as Jayne fussed about, picking up Maggie's bag and the paperwork she'd left on Sam's desk. She looked a bit tired, but that wasn't it.

The spark in her eyes had only gone once before, and that had been at her darkest ebb.

A thought jammed itself into place and stuck. This spontaneous trip to the country was definitely loaded with something heavier than just getting HR off of her back. She'd managed to dodge the village for the past seven years, so... why now?

Jayne waved the paperwork at him. 'All right if I pop in another time to talk through these?'

'Yeah, sure. Absolutely.'

He caught himself smiling. They'd always enjoyed doing that. Going over patients' notes together had been one of the myriad reasons they'd planned to work together. *Live together. Love together.*

Well... He supposed he'd see how much things had changed when she came in. Things he would remind himself of when she left again. Because this wouldn't last. *Couldn't* last. Jayne Sinclair had made it more than clear her future was not in Whitticombe. And not with him.

Jayne bundled Maggie towards the corridor and Sam automatically moved forward to put his hand on the small of Jayne's back. He saw her notice the movement out of the corner of his eye and pulled it away. Which was ridiculous. What were his fingers going to do? Catch on fire if he touched her?

He gave himself a few extra seconds to regroup before going out to the waiting room to get his next patient. Tommy Stark. A ten-year-old boy who looked as though he'd had a bit of a run-in with a fist in the playground.

'Oof. That looks sore.'

'Yup.' Tommy grinned as he followed Sam into his office with his mother in tow.

His mum explained how her son had managed to insert himself between the school bully and the school chess champion, a rather shy girl called Molly.

'That was a brave thing to do,' Sam said.

'Nah,' the little boy explained. 'I did it for love, so it doesn't hurt.'

Sam hid his rueful smirk as he checked the boy over, then showed them out of the room. If only it were that easy.

'Have you gone completely mad?'

A blade of guilt swept through Jayne as words flew out of her mouth and steam poured out of her ears. What was Maggie *thinking*?

The whole point of bedrest was doing just that. Resting. Not pole-vaulting them both straight into the heart of village life.

Maggie was totally unfazed. Perhaps it was the promise of grilled food on the horizon. Or maybe it was the foot-rub Jayne was giving her. The only successful lure to get her active friend to sit down.

'Ow! Not so hard. It's the *cricket*,' Maggie offered amiably in explanation, then pointed to her foot. 'You missed a bit.'

Jayne arched an eyebrow. 'It's not just "the cricket", Mags. It's the whole of freaking Whitticombe coming out to play!'

'So?'

'So... I just...'

She didn't want the entire universe to know she was back. Not *en masse*, anyway. It was hard enough being home at all, let alone at this time of year. Only two short weeks away from the anniversary of the day her sister died. If they knew it had been her fault they'd... Ugh... It didn't bear thinking about.

'It just seems a bit awkward, you know?'

'Why? You're a Whitticomber. So's near enough everyone else. Think of yourself as a stand-in for your parents. Cheer for them, too.'

Her voice softened as she asked, 'How are they, anyway?'

Another blade of guilt sliced through Jayne's conscience. 'They're all right...'

She'd sent a couple of texts, telling them she was going to be staying with Maggie, and had received a short message in return. They were fine. It was quiet. They were both working a lot.

Nothing more personal than her patient notes.

Brief, informative texts seemed to be the only way they could communicate since Jules had died. As if her twin had been the glue that had held them together. Jayne had stayed home for a couple of months afterwards, but whenever they'd looked at her she'd seen the emptiness in their eyes. They all knew but they never spoke the one simple truth.

If Jayne hadn't rung Jules...if Jayne hadn't asked her to ride to the pub...her sister would be alive and well today. If only she'd screamed loud enough. Fast enough.

The sports car had been moving so fast when Jules had whipped round the corner on her bicycle. Jayne's screams had stayed lodged in her throat. When her sister had been pronounced brain-dead it had been as if they would never stop sounding inside her own head.

As best she could, Jayne conjured up a smile and put away the massage cream, rubbing the residue into her hands. The tingle of the minty gel reminded her of how she'd felt when, just for a nanosecond, Sam had reached forward to put his hand on the small of her back as they'd left his office—until he'd caught her noticing and pulled it back. Fire then ice.

'Apparently it's not much of a summer as far as the weather is concerned. They're up in the farthest reaches of the Scottish isles.'

Maggie pulled a face. 'I couldn't live up there. Although I suppose the communities must be close, what with the weather and all. I was talking to the McTavishes—'

Jayne lifted her brow questioningly.

'They're the ones who are doing the house-swap with your parents. Really nice couple. They *love* my kids. Said they don't have grandkids of their own, so they always pounce on a chance to play with them. Mrs McTavish has been teaching Connor how to sketch. It's pretty cool!'

It sounded cool. Just the sort of thing her father would have done with her own children if she'd lived down the road in The Old Barn with Sam, as they'd planned. Bundled a child upon his knee and pulled out a huge sketchpad, as he had done with each of them. Jules had taken to it like a duck to water, but Jayne's artistry had always lain much more firmly in the surgical field. In fixing things.

That was why she spent all her spare time in the other hospital departments. No way would she ever again fall into the 'helpless maiden' category. Not after that horrible day.

Kneeling on the pavement next to Jules after she'd been hit, not caring that her own knees were scraped raw, Jayne had felt so *helpless*. She'd done CPR, but her sister's injuries had been so severe the only thing she'd been able to do was keep her heart beating until someone else had told her otherwise. There had been no way she was going to call her own sister's death.

She hadn't even thought of becoming a surgeon at that point. It had been general practice with a specialty in paediatrics all the way. Sam would do the 'oldies'. She'd look after the little ones. And between the two of them they'd take care of everyone ese. It had been a perfect plan for a perfect life.

'Woo-hoo? Earth to Jayne?' Maggie pulled back and then suddenly went wide-eyed, as if a lightbulb had gone on inside her head.

'You aren't being weird about the cricket because of Sam, are you?'

Jayne made a scoffing noise. 'No.'

'Ohmigawd, you totally *are.*'

She wasn't. Okay. She was. A bit. But what she felt for Sam was just one piece of a bigger puzzle. Something had been ripped open inside her when she'd called Stella's time of death. Something she'd thought had healed.

Maggie gave her belly a double-handed rub. 'You're not still in love with him, are you?'

Jayne did not dignify the question with an answer. Of course a part of her was. Always would be. Their's had been a love that ran so deep it could never be completely erased. Even if she'd told him otherwise.

'Jayne…' Maggie's voice held a warning note. 'If you're here to win Sam's heart again you should tread very, very carefully. The man's been through a lot. His divorce was only a year ago, and of course he's had to cope with his mum passing. He's strong, of course. He's Sam. But—'

'That's *not* why I'm here,' Jayne snapped, a bit too defensively.

She looked into her friend's eyes and saw twenty years of friendship shining back at her. Why was she lying? She knew why she was back. She was here because calling Stella's time of death had made her feel as if she'd killed her sister all over again.

Pain. Anguish. Guilt.

Feelings she wasn't meant to be having. Not as a top surgeon, anyway. She'd thought placing that heart in Stella's body would salve the torment she'd been carrying with her all these years. When Stella's body had rejected the heart Jayne had felt as if it had rejected her too. All of which boiled down to one simple truth: if Jayne didn't find a way to make genuine amends for her sister's death, and the emotional wreckage she'd left in her wake, she could not continue as a surgeon. And that was a future she was completely unwilling to imagine.

Maggie tipped her head to the side, looking not unlike the twelve-year-old version of herself who had befriended Jayne after a particularly rough round of netball. 'Whatever it is that's brought you back... I just want you to know I'm glad you're here. If you ever need to talk...'

It was an offer Maggie had given her countless times. But the only person Jayne had come close to confessing the full story to was Sam. No matter how close she felt to Mags, he'd always been the sounding board she'd needed. He was wise beyond his years. Always gave her perspective on things without making her feel stupid.

When she'd handed him back his ring she'd seen every emotion in his eyes. Pain. Anger. Hurt. Frustration. Disbelief. But instead of lashing out he'd leant in and given her cheek the softest kiss.

'No matter what it is you're going through,' he'd said, 'I want you to know there is a light at the end of the tunnel. You may not see it now, but you will find the way. You'll survive this. Believe me when I say you are so much stronger than you think you are.'

If she had believed him would they be together now?

Back then it had seemed impossible. The only path she'd seen was to pursue her sister's dreams with blinkered, exacting energy. A path so narrow there had been no room for anyone else on it.

It had taken Stella's death to make her realise

just how wrong she'd been. No amount of lives saved would ever bring her sister back.

She forced herself to pop on a smile and clapped her hands together. 'Honestly—I'm good. Just...you know...it's always a little bit weird seeing an ex, right?'

Maggie gave an apologetic shrug and automatically gave her wedding ring, now hanging from a chain around her neck, a quick rub. She wouldn't know. She and Nate had married pretty much straight out of school, before he'd headed off to boot camp. Theirs had been a very similar romance to Jayne and Sam's. Childhood sweethearts making good on their teenage dreams. Well... Not so similar. But Jayne was happy for them.

She cocked her head to the side at the sound of children laughing. 'Why don't I round up those kids of yours and get us to the cricket ground?'

Maggie peered at her for another moment, obviously trying to decide whether or not she should try and force Jayne to talk, and then thought better of it. 'Let's do that. The doctor said I was supposed to keep my calorie consumption up—so bring on the burgers!'

CHAPTER THREE

HALF AN HOUR LATER Jayne was still steeling herself for some sort of retribution.

The beautifully manicured cricket ground was bustling with activity. Sam was nowhere to be seen, so that was a bit of breathing room, and the McTavishes had shown up and were every bit as lovely as Maggie had said. They'd taken Connor and Cailey over to the minis' match, before the main Whitticombe team faced off against the neighbouring village.

The villagers were every bit as nice to her as they were on her annual Christmas visits. Lots of hellos and delighted smiles of surprise. She supposed her usual fleeting visit and toast to the festive season never gave anyone a chance to do much of anything else, but the villagers were loyal.

Sam's family were particularly well known for their huge hearts and charitable ways— Sam's adoption being a case in point. His parents had already had three girls, but Sam's mother—a social worker—had been helping a Fire and Rescue team when they'd found Sam abandoned in a rubbish skip as an infant. They'd never made a big fuss of the fact he was adopted, and she knew Sam's heart burnt bright with love and loyalty for them. From his grandad all the way down to his sister's children.

He had always been aware of how fortunate he was to have found his way into the Crenshaws' lives as the son his adoptive parents had always dreamed of having. And when she and Sam had got together, they'd treated her with as much love and kindness as they did their own children.

She wondered how kind his family would be to her now.

She physically shook the thought away, reminding herself that they, too, had offered nothing but love and support after Jules had died. *She* had been the one to turn away from them.

Well, she was here now, and life had moved on. It was time to try and see the village through fresh eyes.

The clubhouse was festooned with bunting. Of course. This was a village that loved bunting. A few dads were getting the huge barbecues up and running. Clusters of children who weren't in the minis' match were running round playing tag, just as the adults had done as kids.

This was nice. Maybe enough time had passed that some of the rawness of the past had genuinely begun to heal over.

'Jayne Sinclair—is that you?'

Sam's sister Kate appeared in front of her, carrying a huge bowl of potato salad. Behind her was the rest of the Crenshaw clan. Jess and Ali. Their husbands. Their children. Mr Crenshaw and his father Ernest—Sam's grandfather. The family she was meant to have been a part of. The family whose secret potato salad recipe would be tucked away in her head by now if she'd married Sam. Memorised. Cherished.

And just like that the few precious seconds of contentment she'd felt dropped away.

Instinct caught her seeking Sam out amongst the melee. His Irish Wolfhound, Elf, was keeping a watchful eye on him as he lifted one of his nephews onto his shoulders so that he could unhook a bit of bunting that had snagged on the corner of the clubhouse. It was a simple act of kindness, but one that drove home exactly the sort of man he was.

He cared. About the big things, the little

things and everything in between. Her heart almost exploded from the pain of acknowledging that he had always been everything she'd wanted in a man and the only one she couldn't have.

There was no coming back from the catalogue of nightmares she'd put him through. When a girl took a man's ring off her finger and said goodbye she had to mean it. She *had* meant it at the time. Hadn't been able to see the wood for the trees. But now that seven years had split the difference… Only she was too late to make those sorts of amends.

'Jayne?' Sam's sister was looking at her curiously. 'Everything all right? It's good to see you outside your normal visit.'

'Yes…um…' She shook her head distractedly and flicked her thumb over her shoulder. 'I'm here for Maggie. For a few weeks, in fact.'

'Oh, gosh! I hadn't realised.'

Together they looked across to where Maggie appeared to be organising some sort of impromptu three-legged race.

Jayne rolled her eyes and huffed out what she hoped was a comedy sigh. 'She's meant to be *resting*. I'd better go lend her a hand. Get her on to a picnic rug or something.'

And avoid this very awkward conversation.

'Of course.' Kate gave her arm a quick pat. 'And Jayne…just to let you know… Sam's been thinking about dating again, so…' She crinkled her nose and gave her a smile that was hard to interpret. 'Just be careful how you tread if you're back for a bit, yeah? He's already been through a lot.'

A warning. A nice one. But a warning nonetheless.

'Absolutely. Got it.'

She fought a ridiculous impulse to curtsey and instead did what she was brilliant at doing. Turned round and walked away.

'Hey!' Sam ran up behind Jayne as she strode up the small hill that overlooked the pitch. 'Everything okay?'

She whirled round and their eyes caught and locked. Crackles of electricity snapped between them like a summer storm. She stared into his eyes like a deer caught in headlights.

'My sisters said you looked upset. What's going on?'

'What? I'm fine.'

She punched him on the arm. A classic playground flirtation move. Proof, if she needed any, that the plethora of feelings she'd hoped had faded were still alive and kicking.

'Nothing to see here!'

He frowned at her. An uninvited whorl of heat unleashed itself in her belly as goose pimples skittered up her arms.

Sam's frown was kind of sexy. How could she have forgotten how perfectly green his eyes were? That thick, straw-coloured hair…a bit wavy, a bit not. Lightly stubbled cheeks and a jaw that just begged a girl to trace her fingers along it before landing on that remarkably full pair of lips of his.

She pressed her fingers against the rough bark of a tree and dug in, praying it was enough to stop her from wrapping herself around him.

Unexpectedly, he flipped his frown into a variation on a smile. A wary one. But still that same sexy, slow smile that lit her up from the inside out.

He'd never fixed that slight overlap of his two front teeth. Funny how the tiny imperfection made the whole picture perfect.

He hooked his thumbs on his hips. Hips barely holding up a pair of chinos that were only just keeping purchase on the hem of a white shirt that brought out his early summer tan…

Grown-up Sam was…*mmm*…extra-nice. The little crinkles by his eyes and the tiny hints of white hair at his temples unleashed a whole new set of butterflies and fireworks…

Just as quickly they were extinguished.

Those crinkles and the white hair hadn't been there before he'd moved on from their disastrous relationship. Time had taken its toll. Or, more accurately, life. A divorce. The loss of his mother. A pair of body blows there was no proper consolation for. Especially when the divorce had been finalised just a few months before his mother's death.

She wanted to hug him. She *should* hug him. Their shared past held her back.

'Sorry about your…um…you know… Things.'

Sam looked at her long and hard, those green eyes of his boring straight through to her soul. He didn't dignify her paltry commiserations with a response.

She had attended the funeral with her parents but hadn't stayed to pass on her condolences. She regretted that because she *was* sorry for his loss. And for so much more than she would ever be able to stuff into a *Thinking of you at this difficult time* card.

'You planning on hiding up here for the rest of the match or are you actually here to help Maggie?'

The challenging spark in Sam's eyes made mincemeat of the oxygen in her lungs. There was definitely an edge to him now. Something hard and unyielding that she hadn't expected.

He shifted and gave her a look that was almost edged with respect. 'I'm impressed that you came. It's got to be tough. Especially this time of year.'

This time of year. What a loaded phrase.

Fifteen days and about eight hours away from the moment of impact.

She threw on a smile Jules would've given her stamp of approval. The type of grin that said the world might have given her a kick or two, but she was going to keep on keeping on.

'Ha! You and me both, mate.'

They both flinched at the use of the word 'mate'. He'd been her childhood sweetheart. First kiss. First dance. First love. She'd said yes when he'd gone down on bended knee and presented her with a perfect diamond solitaire.

Wept in solitude when she'd returned it. Sam Crenshaw was not a casual buddy.

No matter how many times she'd told herself leaving him was the right thing to do, each time she saw him her heart had begged her to change her mind.

Jayne nodded her head towards the table where Maggie was sitting, receiving the full adoration of the villagers now that news of her tricky pregnancy had spread.

'I've scanned through the notes you gave me. It reads worse than she's acting. How is she really?'

He ticked Maggie's diagnoses off on his fingers. 'Pre-eclampsia. Gestational diabetes. Twin pregnancy. She's on a bit of a tightrope walk, if I'm honest. She's all right now, but...' His voice took on a warning note. 'She won't be if she doesn't start putting her feet up properly. You know as well as I do how quickly these symptoms can take a turn for the worse.'

She did. There was a specialist unit in her hospital for mothers who were experiencing difficult pregnancies. Too many times her colleagues had been forced to call a time of death. She wished now she'd done a few more shadow shifts in that department. Maybe she'd give one of her colleagues a call. Get a few key notes on what to look out for. There wasn't a chance in the universe that Maggie was going downhill on *her* watch.

Jayne gave a jaunty salute to cover up the fact that her insides were jelly. 'Ready and on high alert. My sole remit is to keep those babies right where they belong. And Mum healthy. And, of course, make sure her children eat more than toast. Toast that isn't burnt. Can they *make* toast?'

She was wittering now. She couldn't help it. Sam's entire visage spoke of a man who believed she'd keep her word about as much as he believed in the Tooth Fairy.

He lowered his voice and leant in. She tried her best not to breathe in. One whiff of warm skin and that spicy man scent of his and her knees would start misbehaving.

'She needs this, Jayne. She needs *you*. If you let her down I'll—'

'You'll what?' she challenged.

His voice hardened. 'I'll pick up the pieces. But I will *not* have your back. You'll have to ride this one out on your own.'

She wanted to protest. It wasn't as if being

here was easy for her. If he had even the slightest clue of just how difficult…

Why not tell him? A burden shared...

No. If Sam knew that their engagement had led to her sister's death… No chance. She wasn't letting him take any of the heat for this one. Jules's death was solidly on her. *She'd* been the one who'd agreed to race her sister. She'd been the one who hadn't got Jules's helmet to her on time. The one who hadn't screamed loud enough in warning when that sports car had raced round the corner.

She looked him in the eye. 'I've promised to help. I'll help.'

The crinkles round his eyes narrowed. Enough to send a wash of ice water through her veins.

'Don't you trust me?' she asked quietly.

Sam didn't say anything. He didn't have to. The number of times she'd seen that same flash of emotion in his eyes was the number of times her own heart had broken.

Talk about 'open mouth and insert foot'. She might as well shove both her feet in there and have done with it.

Sam eventually broke the awkward silence. 'I guess you've probably heard the news?'

Her mind reeled for a second, then landed on the most recent thing she'd heard about Sam.

'Yes! Absolutely. Your sister told me. Um… well…good luck with the dating thing!'

Both his eyebrows shot up and he barked a tight laugh. 'That wasn't the news I was talking about. I meant the news that Kate is pregnant again. I saw you two talking.'

Oh. And, *ouch.* No, Kate had only mentioned that she had better watch herself with Sam. Then it hit her. Maybe he hadn't *wanted* her to know about the dating. Her tummy did an involuntary flip.

She sought his eyes for any signs of lingering affection. But just as she sensed those creases by his eyes might be about to soften a pixie-haired woman Jayne didn't recognise swooped in, bearing a pair of wine glasses.

'*There* you are, Sam! I wondered where you'd got to. I thought we were going to sit down by the pitch? Hope it wasn't too cheeky, but I've brought you a glass of Pinot from the bar. Mmm! Delicious. I am *parched.* So…' The woman—petite, blonde, and with huge fawn eyes—looked at Jayne then back at Sam. 'Friend of yours?'

'Something like that,' Sam said, his eyes still glued to Jayne's. 'Blast from the past.'

Another burst of fireworks exploded in Jayne's belly. *That was one way to put it.*

Sam shifted his weight and touched the woman's arm. 'Jayne Sinclair—allow me to introduce you to Nell Pace.'

Her heart sank straight to her toes. Sam wasn't *considering* dating. He was *on a date.*

The fireworks went out in one swift move.

'Hi! Goodness… Well!' Jayne's voice was getting a bit screechy. 'Nice to meet you.'

Sam threw her a peculiar look as Nell launched into an explanation as to how they'd met.

'My aunt works with Sam. I'm new in the village and she thought we'd hit it off, so when I heard about the cricket match I thought I'd come along and say hello.'

Sam looked about as uncomfortable as Jayne felt. So Jayne did the only thing she could think of to fix it.

Scarper.

She threw a frantic wave in Maggie's direction. 'I really should get going. Maggie's waiting for me, and I'm the last person to stand in the way of a budding…um…friendship…'

She was. Absolutely she was. But if she hadn't been cringing before, she was properly mortified now. It was as if she were wearing an invisible scarlet letter on her chest. *A for Abandonment.* If only it were absolution.

Nell waved one of those fingertip waves as Sam, who was now standing behind Nell, gave Jayne a quick nod that said a thousand things.

First and foremost it said *Don't you dare let Maggie down.* He was watching her.

Her heart suddenly weighed about a million pounds. It looked as if Whitticombe wasn't the time machine she'd thought it might be after all.

Jayne slammed the ladies' room door shut and headed straight to the sink. She threw cold water on her face, willing it to help the heat fade from her cheeks.

She'd known coming back would be tough, but talk about out of the frying pan and into the fire!

She caught her own eye in the mirror and saw things through the chinks in her armour that she barely wanted to acknowledge. Loneliness. Loss.

Maybe you don't want to be alone as much as you think you do. Maybe that's why you came back here instead of running even further away.

She quelled a frustrated howl and stamped her foot. She was living the life she wanted to live. The life her sister couldn't. If that meant sucking it up in London and trying to do the things her adrenaline junkie sister would normally have had to beg her to do, so be it.

So she didn't like bungee jumping? She could get over that. And the constant hum and buzz of city life. And the late night clubbing. And, and, and…

What she *did* love was her job. While there were no silver linings in losing Jules, her sister's death had brought out a love for paediatric surgery Jayne would have never known she had. She genuinely, one hundred per cent, loved what she did for a living.

Which begged the question why had she come running back to Whitticombe instead of perfecting her techniques at the hospital?

Helping children at their most vulnerable moments was one of the most rewarding things in the world. *Except when it wasn't.*

The truth brought streaks of red to her cheeks.

Losing Stella had thrown her right back to that day when she'd lost her sister. And feeling that level of pain and loss meant being in Whitticombe. So here she was dodging her ex—in the loo.

Now what? Stay in here until everyone had gone home?

Hardly.

She blinked away a couple of tears and forced her brain to take part in the conversation.

Losing Stella was a loss…but not a failure. She knew that intellectually. Her heart took a nose-dive as memories flooded in. But losing Stella with *that* particular heart and then crying about it… That was proof—as if she needed any—that she was still wrestling with her sister's death.

She forced herself to look at the mirror again. She'd sometimes pretend she was looking into Jules's eyes when she looked into her reflection. Sometimes she genuinely thought she caught glimpses of her. Especially when she was scrubbing in for surgery. They'd been identical twins, after all.

But lately it had been harder to drum up that vital, energy-charged version of herself. The version that was part Jayne and part Jules. She had no idea who she was looking at right now.

Seven years was a long time to keep a ghost alive.

She stuck her tongue out at her reflection, then forced a silly grin. She was here for Maggie. Sure, it might not have started out that way, but it was a chance to prove she could do something good in the world.

An image of Sam's dubious expression popped into her head. She quickly shook it away.

Six weeks. She could do just about anything for six weeks.

She pushed through the door, determined to make a better go of it, and bashed straight into a chest. A chest that smelt of grass and wood and a kick of grapefruit as the perfect olfactory chaser.

In other words it was a chest that smelt of Sam Crenshaw.

Couldn't a girl get five minutes on her own to wrestle with her past?

Trying to keep her voice light—fun, even—Jayne looked up into those green eyes of his and joked, 'Look, Sam, I know I don't have a great track record in sticking around, but I'm pretty sure you can count on me not to climb out through the window of the ladies' loo.'

He tilted his chin to the side and gave her a confused look. 'I was just checking that you were all right. You looked upset.'

Score one to Sam for still being able to read her emotional barometer.

But she couldn't accept sympathy from him. Not with her yo-yoing emotions.

'Aw... You wanted to make sure my heart wasn't breaking because you're on a date? Don't you worry. I'm not jealous.'

Sam's arched eyebrow made a reappearance.

Oh, sugar. She was *totally* jealous.

If Jayne could have thrown herself into the world's deepest pool of quicksand she would have done it. Immediately.

She pulled her ponytail across her eyes, unwilling to read what was going on in Sam's. 'Sorry...sorry. I'm happy for you. Of all the people in the universe, you deserve happiness.'

'And you don't?'

She dropped her ponytail and felt it swish between her shoulder blades as her eyes met Sam's.

Now, *that* was a loaded question.

His eyebrow dropped back into place. His tight smile softened. He lifted his hand up and swept the backs of his fingers against her cheek.

Against everything her brain was screaming at her to do, she leant into them. A cardinal sin if ever there was one.

Sparks flooded her bloodstream and her heart bashed against her ribcage so hard she was sure the unicorn on her T-shirt looked as if it was galloping. Not that she could tear her eyes away from his and check. It might have been raining diamonds at this very moment and she wouldn't have noticed.

'Miss me?' he asked softly.

'Yeah…' She only just managed to deadpan. 'Something *awful.*'

She did actually. Always had. More than she'd ever admit. To *him* anyway. Each Christmas at the pub she'd seek out his dog, Elf, and whisper it into his ear. Elf always licked her nose as if he got it.

Sam took a step closer towards her.

'How much?'

Her heart skipped a beat. And then quite a few more. She hadn't been this close to Sam in years. Being touched by him…her body wanting nothing more than to be just that little bit closer…they were just the beginning of a myriad reasons why coming home had never been on her to-do list.

She felt the space between the two of them diminish.

Maybe it was the failed surgery. Maybe it was seeing him with another woman. Maybe it was the simple fact that she'd loved Sam Crenshaw for near enough her entire life and being here with him and not touching him was next to impossible.

They were going to kiss. She could see it in the angle of his chin. Feel it in his fingers on hers. Her heels lifting off the ground so she could reach his mouth.

Just as her feet felt as if they were going to begin floating Sam pulled back. He scrubbed his hands through his hair and looked about as confused as she felt.

What had *that* been about? Another test?

If it had been an experiment to see if there were still a few sparks flying between them, Jayne was pretty sure they had the answer to that.

'I'm guessing that wasn't meant to happen.' Jayne made a couple of comedy noises to show Sam she was willing to pretend it had never happened if he was.

He cleared his throat and rubbed his hand along the back of his neck. 'Right, um…'

Sam didn't seem to know which way to look. Anywhere but at her seemed to be working for him.

'I was just on my way to put some orders in at the bar. Want anything?'

'No, I'd better not. I'm driving Maggie and the children back.'

When he turned around she skimmed her fingers across her lips, as if they had actually been bruised by the kisses that never came, then scraped the sensation away with her nails.

She watched as he strode swiftly to the bar, taking note of all the waves and back-slaps and hellos he received on the way. Just like his father and grandfather before him, he was a valued member of the community. Someone people respected. Someone people loved. Someone they'd protect...

All of the sudden the low hum of activity from the playing field burst into cries of dismay, quickly followed by loud calls for Sam.

Sam ran as fast as he could. Faster when he saw it was his grandad lying stretched out at the far end of the cricket pitch.

Calls to clear the area and to give Ernest some air wrapped round him as he knelt down by his grandfather, who was trying to push himself up to seating.

'It's all right, Sammy. It's just a sprained ankle.'

Sam knew his grandad wasn't critically injured, but the wince and the quick breaths he was taking told him the seventy-eight-year-old had taken a proper fall.

Ernest gave his wrist a tentative back-and-forth bend which indicated that would need a look as well. If he'd been looking up into the air for the cricket ball, then tripped and stumbled, he definitely would've used his wrists to blunt the fall.

Sam sat back on his heels and grinned. 'What sort of stunt move was it this time, Grandad? Did you think you were playing for England today?'

His grandfather waved him off and reached out to pull up his trouser cuffs. His knees weren't stained green, which meant they hadn't taken any of his weight either. At his age there were also his hips to think about. Bone infection if there was a break. Nerve or blood vessel damage. Arthritis.

It was a long list.

Sam was just about to start in on the stream

of questions that followed an injury like this when he felt rather than saw Jayne kneeling by his side and sliding a first aid kit into place between them.

His grandad's eyes brightened.

Despite the intense moment they'd shared earlier, Sam found it strangely reassuring to have her there. Sure, it wasn't a critical injury, but Sam had cared for his mother whilst she was dying of cancer and that had been tough. A blunt reminder of exactly why doctors treating their own family was not a good thing.

It made his heart stop for a moment as he reminded himself that Jayne had been all on her own when her sister had been struck by that sports car. She must have been absolutely terrified. He'd been over and over the scenario a million times and it always ended the same way. With a diamond ring in his hand.

Had he been so blinded by the way she'd shut him out that he'd genuinely not realised how helpless she'd felt?

His family had drawn even closer together during his mother's illness. The opposite had happened to Jayne's. As if the injuries Jules had sustained had had a ripple effect. Little wonder... They'd had no time to prepare.

As awful as it had been to see his mother so ill, they'd had time to prepare. To attack her bucket list. To say they loved her and to say goodbye. Jayne and her parents hadn't had any of that. The world as they'd known it had changed in the blink of an eye.

'Jayne? What on earth are you doing here?' Ernest dropped her a wink, then winced. 'They didn't drop you in from some sort of helicopter ambulance, did they?'

'Oh, no—that's the sort of thing my sister would—' She stopped and gave her head a short shake. 'I've brought along the cricket club's first aid kit. Someone mentioned a stretcher and they're having a dig around for that.' She made a quick scan though the medical kit. 'I'm guessing we should start with some ice packs.' She held one out to Sam. 'Shall I play nurse to your doctor?'

It should have been a loaded question. She was a surgeon. He was a GP. In this scenario this kind of injury was his proverbial bread and butter. But Sam knew Jayne wasn't pulling any sort of rank. Injuries like this needed to be treated quickly.

Sam's grandad might have been born and raised in the heart of World War II—and might be the poster boy for stiff upper lips—but he was going pretty pale. It was easy to see they needed to get him to hospital for a thorough check.

'Are we going to go straightforward P-R-I-C-E on this one?'

Sam nodded. *Protect, rest, ice, compress and elevate.* The easiest and most effective guidelines for a minor soft tissue injury. 'There are no obvious breaks. Not from what I've seen. Want to double-check his ankle for me?'

'I hope you two aren't forgetting I *am* actually a doctor,' Ernest piped up.

'Not at all,' said Jayne. 'You're the reason I wanted to become one in the first place.'

Sam smiled and accepted a stretchy bandage to wrap round his grandad's wrist.

He remembered when Jayne's mum had used to bring bright flushes of red to her daughter's cheeks as she told the story of Jayne bringing a cloth dolly to the doctor's surgery as a little girl. She and Jules had become embroiled in a tug of war and the doll had been its victim. Her little cloth hand had been torn off and Jayne had been inconsolable. Ernest had taken the doll, put it on the exam table and asked it a few questions. Then carefully inserted an IV before pulling the curtain round him while he deftly stitched the hand back on and handed the doll to Jayne as good as new.

He refocused on his grandfather's wrist. 'The way the swelling's ballooning on your wrist, Grandad, I'm afraid you're going to need an X-ray.'

'The ankle as well,' Jayne said apologetically as she gingerly lifted his grandfather's foot.

The exposed area between his trousers and his sock was already visibly swollen, and taking on some rather unnatural hues.

'I'm just going to take your shoe off, if that's all right?'

''Course it is! I'd do it myself if my grandson here would quit his fussing over my wrist. It's only—*ouch!*' He pulled his arm protectively to his chest. 'Well…maybe an X-ray would be a good idea.'

After a couple of men had shown up with the stretcher, and they'd rolled his grandfather on to his side to load him up, Ernest began grumbling—a good sign that his injuries weren't too serious.

'I have a load of patients on the roster tomorrow,' he protested. 'So the sooner we sort this the better.'

Sam barked a laugh. 'You're not going anywhere near a patient for at least a week.'

'What?' Ernest squawked. 'There is *no* chance you can run that surgery on your own.'

Sam got ready to launch into a well-rehearsed speech about how he'd been getting himself up to speed for the past three years so he could do precisely that. He would leave out the part about how they had always meant for there to be two of them in the surgery. But before he could say anything Jayne's voice filled a brief lull in the general hubbub.

'I could help.'

He felt as if the entire village had taken a collective breath. Of course it wasn't true, but as most of the people here knew their history it felt that way.

'You've already got Maggie to look after—and the children.' If there was a grateful way to wave off an offer of help he hoped he was doing it.

She shrugged. She clearly wasn't going to push it.

'Fair enough. But Maggie lives three doors down from the surgery. I'm pretty sure I could run down any time you need me.' She pulled her mobile phone out of her pocket. 'I think that's what these are for.'

Sam was about to protest again, but before he could say anything Jayne put her hands up.

'Don't worry about it. Just saying... The offer's there if you need it.'

Then she walked away.

It was a view he should be used to. And not in a sexy way as her thighs and bum swished against the fabric of her skirt, either.

He never should have touched her. Feeling the soft skin of her cheek had brought back countless good memories when he should be focusing on the bad ones. The reasons they weren't meant to be together.

'It's all right, Grandad. I can hold the fort for a few weeks if necessary.' Before his grandfather could protest he added, 'It'll only be a week if they really are just sprains. Two at most.'

His grandfather shook his head. 'You've had an offer of help, son. You'd be a damn fool not to take it.'

Sam knew what he was saying. It was hard to admit to needing help. But sometimes you simply had to do it.

If only Jayne had accepted *his* offers accepting hers now would be a moot point...because she'd already be by his side.

CHAPTER FOUR

A FEW HOURS into his work day and Sam was regretting refusing Jayne's offer. His grandfather had sustained a fracture in his wrist and a sprain in his ankle. The fractured wrist meant he would be off work for a few weeks, whether he liked it or not. Their patients' care was first and foremost and a doctor in a sling wasn't ideal.

Greta, the surgeon's long-time receptionist, was run off her feet, trying to reschedule nonurgent patients and Sam was trying to dispense with the 'take all the time you need' philosophy he prided himself on.

He jotted down a couple of numbers then turned to his current patient. 'The blood pressure pills definitely seem to be doing the trick, Mrs Greenfield.'

'No!'

Sam laughed. Denial wasn't the usual response he got when something was going according to plan. He turned the blood pressure monitor towards his sixty-something patient. 'See for yourself. Lowest blood pressure you've had in years.'

'I can see it well enough, Sam. My eyesight's never been the problem. Oops. Sorry. *Dr Crenshaw.*' The grey-haired woman tittered at her mistake. 'I'm still just so used to your grandfather being the only Dr Crenshaw in town.'

'I've been your doctor for three years now, Mrs Greenfield,' Sam reminded her playfully.

'I know…but you're also the same little boy who used to mow my lawn.'

Sam grinned. 'If memory serves, I'm *still* the same boy who mows your lawn.'

Mrs Greenfield smiled. 'Yes… You've been good to me since I lost my Daniel.'

She gave a quiet little sigh and pressed her hands to her heart. Her husband had died some fifteen years ago and she still wore her… *Wait a minute.* Where was her wedding ring?

As if she'd read his mind, Mrs Greenfield turned her focus to her hands as she wove her bare fingers together on her lap. 'Dr Crenshaw, I'm curious. Do you think that, rather than the pills, *love* might have something to do with lower blood pressure?'

'Love?' This appointment wasn't going in the direction he'd anticipated.

Mrs Greenfield nodded, but didn't meet his eye.

Love as an antidote to high blood pressure? *His* blood pressure had just about shot off the scale when Jayne had walked into his office yesterday. Double that when they'd nearly kissed. He didn't know what sort of divine intervention had pulled him back from that mistake, but… It was a path best left unexplored.

'I'm taking it from your silence, Dr Crenshaw, that there is no scientific evidence to suggest that love might lower blood pressure?'

'Apologies, Mrs Greenfield.' He scribbled a few numbers on a notepad to make it look as though he'd been doing some calculations. 'Your question caught me off guard.'

'Made you think of romance, did it?' Mrs Greenfield teased, and then she pushed the blood pressure cuff towards Sam. 'Should we be checking out *your* stats? From what I hear, things were very lively at the cricket ground last night.'

Sam suddenly saw where this was going and did his best to steer the conversation in another direction. 'Jayne is back in town to look after Maggie. Nothing to do with me.'

Mrs Greenfield's looked perplexed. 'Jayne? Jayne Sinclair's back in town? I was talking about Greta's niece—Nell. The shy one? Greta was telling me all about it before my appointment.'

Terrific. Greta was the most proactive contributor to the Whitticombe grapevine. And Nell had clearly not passed on to her aunt the 'I'm not really in the market for a relationship' talk he'd had with her when she'd suggested they have a second drink. It had been a white lie on his part, but one he'd thought would protect them both.

'Yes…well…it's always nice to show someone new about town.'

Mrs Greenfield sat back in her chair. 'Ooh, Jayne Sinclair… Now, that takes me back to when I heard that awful screech of tyres just outside on the lane.'

Sam didn't need to ask for embellishment. Mrs Greenfield was talking about the day Jayne's sister had been killed. Things like that didn't happen all that often in Whitticombe, so when they did the scars ran deep. Too deep, in Jayne's case. But he hadn't been there. Didn't know first-hand what she'd been through. He'd certainly treated enough retired servicemen to know that watching someone die wasn't just something you forgot about.

'Such a shame, that was,' Mrs Greenfield continued. 'Her poor parents… How they soldiered on here in Whitticombe is beyond me. I would've moved if I were in their shoes. Would never have been able to set foot in this village ever again.'

A lightbulb pinged on in Sam's head. A few months after Jules had died, Jayne had announced that she wanted to become a paediatric cardiologist. She'd said the only way to pursue her dreams was to live in London. He'd been utterly thrown, because she'd always wanted to be a GP and paediatrician right here in this very surgery.

He'd taken what she'd said at face value. As a slight, even. As if she'd been saying that living in Whitticombe equated to settling for second best rather than seeing it as he did—total life fulfilment. Whitticombe had everything the two of them had valued. Family, friends, a strong community that came together in time of crisis. There were hospitals nearby if Jayne wanted to pursue more advanced paediatric care. Research facilities in Oxford. But mostly…it was *home*.

A community, family and friends Jayne had closed the door on when she would surely have needed them most.

Had he been focusing on the wrong thing all these years? Had Jayne been running from the nightmare of her sister's death rather than pursuing a dream?

That look of pain in her eyes when he'd asked her whether she thought she deserved happiness… Had Jayne been punishing herself all these years?

It had been an accident. Yes…an accident that she would be constantly reminded of every time she came home.

Half of him wanted to pull Mrs Greenfield up into his arms and kiss her. The other half wondered why it had taken him so long to see something so obvious.

'So…about this love theory of mine…'

'Yes. Sorry, Mrs Greenfield.' Sam scrubbed a hand through his hair, hoping it would release all the Jayne-centric thoughts and allow him to concentrate on his patient. 'What's this theory?'

'Well…' She threw him a coy look. 'I have

been enjoying visits from a certain gentleman caller lately.'

Sam's eyebrows shot up. 'Oh?'

Mrs Greenfield's cheeks pinked up. 'It's nothing too racy, Sam. Don't worry.'

He wasn't worried. He was delighted for her. If a bit surprised. He'd thought Mrs Greenfield to be a one-man kind of woman. The same way his father was and his grandfather before him had been. Crenshaw men seemed to pick a woman early on, set his heart at her feet and then get about the business of loving her for the rest of their lives.

Sam gave his jaw a scrub. He obviously wasn't quite as successful as his forebears. It probably worked better when the woman you loved was a willing participant.

'So, who's this fancy man of yours, then?'

'Oh, Sam. He's no fancy man!' Mrs Greenfield chided. 'He's a *gentle*man.'

The way her voice and features softened spoke volumes. She was in love.

'And may I ask how you met this gentleman?'

Her cheeks flushed a soft pink. 'Oh! Well, we were sweethearts back in the day.'

'What? I thought you and Daniel had been an item from the get-go.'

'Oh, no. Not at all. I had what they used to call "a past".'

'Mrs Greenfield! You're shocking me.'

She batted at the air between them. 'Oh, you... I am not. It was nothing, really. Just a flirtation in the school playground. It never amounted to anything. Not back then, anyway. Flirtations were definitely much more conservative back in those days.'

Despite the patients waiting out in Reception, Sam's curiosity overrode the ten-minute window he was supposed to have for each patient. 'So...how did he go from being a bit of a playground Lothario to the gentleman who's lowered your blood pressure?'

'The Lothario's name is Colin.' Her gaze went a little soft focus and dreamy. 'Colin was ambitious back then. *Very* ambitious. Big plans. Big dreams. He didn't want to stay in the tiny little village where we'd grown up and I did. So...he went off to seek his fortune.'

'And came back to Whitticombe to claim it?'

'Something like that.' Mrs Greenfield laughed. 'It wasn't Whitticombe. Smaller, if you can imagine. Anyway, Colin moved all over the world. Made his fortune. Lost it. And his family.' She leant forward and explained, 'His wife turned out to be a bit of a fair weather wife. She didn't like Poor Colin as much as she liked Rich Colin. Anyway!' She swept Colin's past into the bin with a flick of her hand. 'He's started again. New business. New lifestyle choices. New girlfriend.' She made a *ta-da* gesture with her hands.

There were about a thousand things Sam wanted to examine from Mrs Greenfield's story. The childhood romance. The pursuit of dreams. The lessons learnt. The love that was given a second chance. The trust it must take to believe he'd stick around.

Trust.

There it was. The elephant in the room, standing between him and Jayne. He didn't trust her to stay. She didn't trust him to give her the life she wanted.

A perfect impasse.

Sam did his own version of flicking his romantic failures into the bin, opting to stick to his patient's needs. He made a few notes and came to a decision. 'I think we can thank Colin for this.' He ripped up the prescription for more blood pressure pills he'd started making earlier.

'Looks like it.' Mrs Greenfield beamed, then patted his hand. 'Do help Greta transport all those cakes and stews queuing up in Reception to your grandfather, won't you?'

Sam smiled and nodded. Village hospitality at its finest.

He stood, and as he did so Mrs Greenfield said, 'Sam, you know we're all here for you, don't you? In whatever way you need.'

He did. But he wasn't about to fall on his romance sword in front of the entire village again. Not with Jayne anyway. Maybe not ever again.

Butterflies were swooping all around her tummy as Jayne walked down the Victorian tiled corridor to the second door on the right, as Greta had instructed her. She'd come for entirely professional reasons, but everything about being home felt personal.

Home.

What a loaded word.

She started as she heard that rich, all too familiar voice come through the door, then trickle down her spine like warm honey. Her fingers drifted up to her un-kissed lips and, despite trying not to remember just how much she had wanted it, she swept out her tongue to soothe the heat away.

'Come on in, Maggie. Why aren't you putting your feet—?' Sam pulled open the door and stopped dead in his tracks when his eyes met Jayne's. 'Ah. It's you.'

Not quite the response she'd been hoping for, but she supposed it was a response she should get used to. He was moving on with his life… and she was a blip from his past.

Sam crossed his arms over her chest. His lovely, warm, solid chest.

'What are you doing here?'

Okay. Someone's bedside manner could do with a bit of work today.

'I brought some cake for your grandad. Don't worry. I didn't make it.'

'Jayne. It's incredibly busy and you know you could've just brought it to the house. Why are you here?'

Swallowing back a sharp retort that went something along the lines of *I told you I would help but you refused in front of everyone*, she said, 'I wanted to go over Maggie's notes with you, *as she requested*, but if you're too busy I can just ring some nameless, faceless person at the hospital.'

Sam ushered her in. 'Apologies.' He didn't

sound all that sorry. 'I— The appointment was in Maggie's name so I was surprised, that's all.'

He looked tired. He hadn't shaved. The mix of gold and auburn stubble suited him, but she could tell by the way he scrubbed at it uncomfortably that he wasn't used to it.

'How's your grandad?'

'Good. Well, sore and bruised, and already driving my sisters batty, but… It's a fracture in his wrist and a sprained ankle. He'll be the size of a house if he eats all the cakes that have been flooding in.'

Jayne stifled a laugh as she thought of Sam's sisters flying round Ernest, tending to him with all the fuss and bother Sam's mum had been so good at. They were a family of natural comforters. Unlike her own who—when tested— had discovered that they preferred to lick their wounds in private.

Or maybe you sent yourself to purgatory and didn't give them a chance.

She sat down in the chair Sam hadn't yet suggested she sat in even though she was pretty sure that's how the whole doctor-patient thing worked. *Come in. Sit down. How may I help you?*

Sam let his chair accept his full weight and

started tapping away on his computer. He had yet to meet her eyes again.

Her heart split wide open for him. She got it. Having her show up out of the blue had to be awful for him. If the tables had been turned she probably would've run away.

Just like you did after Jules died.

No. She hadn't run away. She'd changed. Doggedly poured her energies, her determination…her *grief*…into becoming the best paediatric cardio surgeon she could. One who could do transplants, so that the next time she was in a seemingly impossible situation she could do something about it.

A sick feeling washed through her as she thought of Stella's grief-stricken parents. The loss they must be feeling because of her.

The organ didn't take. It wasn't your fault.

She desperately wanted to talk it out with someone. And not just any anyone. She wanted to talk it out with Sam. He would get it. When they'd started out in med school they'd used to talk on the phone for hours about just that very thing. The cruel randomness of illness. The limits of medicine. The power of talking things through.

He doesn't want to talk to you.

Sam tapped his desk. Presumably so that she would get on with it. She closed her eyes to regroup and opened them just in time to see him lick his lips.

Damn, the man was sexy. She crossed her legs again and sat up straight.

His eyes flicked up to the wall clock. 'Jayne…? There's a waiting room full of patients—what do you want?'

She pulled a notebook from her tote bag. 'I wanted to get your take on everything Maggie's been experiencing. I've read the hospital notes, but I thought you'd know better than her part-time doctor there.'

'Or her part-time friend?'

Ouch!

The barbed words had hit their mark. This definitely wasn't going to be the breezy chit-chat about Maggie's health she'd been hoping for.

'We text. *And* email.'

Sam's lips thinned.

Fine. She could have been a better friend. Come home more regularly. Not counted on pure happenstance to put her in Maggie's path when she needed her most.

Questions flooded in where she should have had answers.

What if she'd stayed? What if she'd finally opened up to her parents, Sam—everyone—and admitted what she and she alone knew. That she was responsible for her sister's death.

If she had stayed…and by some miracle been forgiven…she might be married now. To Sam. Maybe even have children of her own. But that was a big *if*. Before forgiveness must come the courage to admit her failures. Failures that gnawed at her conscience every single day.

She was alive. Her sister wasn't. And there was no one else in the world who could make her sister's dreams come true.

She pressed her hands to her face and peeked at Sam through her fingers. If only she was brave enough to tell him her deepest, darkest secret.

She rubbed her fingers along her closed eyes and saw flashes of light where she usually saw her sister, flying round the corner from their small lane to the larger one…a mane of jet-black hair flying in her wake…the oncoming rush of a yellow sports car.

If she was going to do this—stay here, help

Maggie, not fight with Sam—she was going to have to fall on her sword.

'Sam…' She dropped her hands, trying to control the waves of emotion ricocheting around her insides. 'I know I hurt you—'

He huffed out a humourless laugh. '*I'm* not the one we're talking about here.'

'I think we are,' she countered. 'If you don't trust me to do what's best for Maggie then this is going to be really difficult.'

His eyes flashed bright. She knew what they were saying. He didn't trust her. He was braced for her to be difficult. He was braced for her to leave again.

Something deep inside her—something so deep she rarely let herself acknowledge it— surged into her heart. *Longing.* A longing to bring about that soft look that used to pour through his features when he turned and saw her. The complicit wink he'd used to throw her way that only she had understood. The smile she knew was especially for her.

Her fingers instinctively moved to her lips and shifted across them.

'Can you not do that, please?' Sam shifted uncomfortably in his chair and looked away.

'What?'

'Touch your lips like that.'

'Well, then you shouldn't have almost kissed me,' she snapped, instantly regretting it.

His features hardened. 'I think it was the other way round, actually.'

She was the one who'd gone up on tiptoe. He was the one who'd sought her out in the first place.

Doing her best not to sound defensive, she looked Sam straight in the eye. 'Let's focus on Maggie, shall we? I'm here today. I will be here tomorrow. And the next day and the next. I will be here right up until Maggie has those babies. Longer if need be.'

Sam shook his head and waved his hands for her to stop. 'Jay…'

Her heart leapt to her throat. He hadn't called her plain old Jay in years. 'Yes?'

When he met her eyes again she caught a glimpse of all the heartache she had caused, and then, in the blink of an eye, it was gone. 'Look. You're partly right. About *"the moment"* yesterday.'

At least he was admitting it was a moment.

He looked down at his desk and continued. 'I shouldn't have come after you. You looked upset. Gut instinct kicked in. But… I should've let you be. You're your own boss now.'

A lead weight hit her gut like a wrecking ball. *Wow.* That stung. She was too late even to win his friendship. Had something happened between yesterday and today that had turned him so hard?

Yes, you idiot. The moment.

'Why did you do it? Follow me?'

'I wanted to see if anything was still there.'

It was about as honest an answer as a girl could ask for.

From the look on his face, he regretted the admission. As they were being so blunt she decided to get the whole truth, whether she liked his response or not.

'And was there?'

Sam scrubbed his hand across his chin, then fixed her with a look she would never forget. It was hard, unforgiving and set in stone.

'No. Nothing.'

Then he turned to his computer, printed out a few contact numbers at the nearby hospital in Oxford, handed the piece of paper to her and suggested she call Maggie's obstetrician in future.

Well, then, she thought numbly as she left his office, at least she knew where she stood.

Three days later Sam was still kicking himself for being so awful to Jayne.

Sure. She'd broken his heart back in the day. She had also apologised. Countless times. None of them had ever stuck because he'd never truly believed she was following her heart.

Maybe it was time to believe it. It had been seven years. If the medical journals he'd accidentally-on-purpose pored through were to be believed, she'd hit some stellar professional heights. You didn't work at the London Merryweather because you were in a slump. You worked there because you had a dream. Of being the best.

An image of the hurt lancing through Jayne's eyes popped into his head so vividly he sucked in a sharp breath. Emotion had got the better of him. He'd needed to make a point. Re-draw that line in the sand.

But there had been no need to be so cruel. Or to lie.

He'd felt something. Of *course* he'd felt something. That same old surge of flame licking at everything that made him a man had hit hard

and fast the second her lips were within cen-
timetres of his own. And it had hurt. He had
wanted to feel nothing.

But no amount of hurt should reduce him
to lashing out at a person for a nanosecond's
pleasure. And he hadn't even got that. If anything, the hurt he'd caused her had only made
him feel worse.

Which was why he was standing outside
Maggie's house with a basketful of truce croissants. Jayne's favourite. At least they had been
back in the day.

He rang the bell and half considered leaving
them on the stone doorstep, before reminding
himself that grown men didn't run away from
self-made conflict. Grown men took calculated
risks...with a bit of a buffer if they needed a
quick escape.

*Offer gift. Apologise. Agree to move on. Go
back to surgery where there's a ton of paperwork to tackle. Get on with life.*

Easy-peasy.

The second Jayne opened the door he instantly knew his plan had flaws. The Jayne
standing in the doorway of the chocolate box
cottage was the Jayne he'd fallen in love with.

Her inky black hair was falling free from a

pair of messy topknots. Her bright blue eyes were made up all smoky and mysterious. Her nose was painted black and she had a full set of cat whiskers fanning out across her cheeks, as well as a pair of bright red lips. A curve-hugging cat suit with a zipper that sat just below that delicious divot at the base of her throat and ran right the way down to her belly button completed the outfit.

'Interesting look.' Not really the opening gambit he'd been going for, but...

She looked confused for a minute, then realised he was referring to her face. 'Ha! Yes. Um...the kids and I were having a bit of a practice session this morning and I got distracted. Did you know having children in the house equals about nineteen times the amount of laundry I'm used to?'

She looked nervous. Bracing herself for a repeat of their last fractious encounter, no doubt.

'Are you planning on spending the summer as a house cat?'

Whether she said yes or no, she looked completely endearing. And very, very sexy.

'We were going to put on a play for Maggie. Ears.' She pointed to her topknots and then to the kitchen table, where an array of children's costumes were spread out. 'They dressed me up this morning, while Maggie was having a lie-in. I thought I'd go through the children's costumes while they were at school to see if I could come up with something inspired.'

'Apart from doing your own version of *Cats*?'

'Ha! No. I think you'll remember my singing voice is more like a feral cat than an opera singer. Maggie's the only one with talent in that department.'

She opened the lower half of the barn-style door and stood to the side so he could duck under the thick beam of a doorframe and come into the kitchen.

She pointed at her face. 'This was Cailey's handiwork. I let her raid Maggie's amateur dramatics make-up box before school. To help alleviate the boredom.'

'Cailey's or Maggie's?'

Jayne laughed. 'Maggie's. Definitely Maggie's.'

'She's bored already? I thought she'd be thrilled to tackle a few boxsets.'

He didn't really. Maggie was *always* doing something. Experimenting with new cake flavours for the tearoom. Setting up the village fete. Cheering on her husband at the annual

Whitticombe river football match. When her obstetrician had rung Sam and recommended Maggie be put on bedrest for the final few weeks of her pregnancy, the first words Maggie had uttered were 'House arrest, you mean.'

Jayne cracked a proper smile this time. The type that could put a movie star to shame. Resisting that smile was like stopping time. Impossible.

'Last night she started watching online videos to teach herself how to crochet, because she's already knitted three new baby blankets.'

'What? Since last week?'

Jayne leant against the wooden kitchen counter and drew her top teeth over her lower lip. 'You might not know this, but Maggie doesn't really do relaxation all that well.'

Sam was about to say he was pretty sure he knew Maggie better than Jayne did, seeing as he saw her near enough every day, then stopped himself. He wasn't here to nark. He was here to offer an olive branch. Not stare at her teeth, or her lips, or her adorable button nose.

Big breath in...big breath out.

That was something he hadn't had to do in a while. The old trick of counting down until he'd made sure he wouldn't say something he was going to regret. His grandad had taught him that one when he'd had one too many patients asking to see 'the *grown-up* Dr Crenshaw...'

Three...two...one.

Coming here was meant to return him to an even keel, not throw him further off-course. Three days of trying to pretend Jayne wasn't in town had shredded his relaxed demeanour to bits.

He had hurt her with his unnecessary—and untrue—remark about having felt nothing when they had nearly kissed. Of *course* he'd felt something. He'd felt *everything*. And that was precisely why he'd denied it. Because for every ounce of pleasure he felt when he was with Jayne, he felt an equal serving of pain.

As if they'd made a decision to move on from small talk about Maggie, Jayne gave a shrug and pointed at his hand. 'What's in your basket, Goldilocks? Are you stealing things from your grandad's growing pile of get-well baked goods?'

'Believe it or not...' He lifted up the basketful of croissants. 'These are expressly for you.'

'Really?' She shot him a look of disbelief as she accepted the basket and inhaled deeply. 'Did you get these at the Vanilla Bean Bakery?'

'Is there anywhere else to buy croissants in Whitticombe?'

He wasn't going to tell her about Carla's raised eyebrows when he'd ordered them. Sam had near enough kept her bakery afloat back in the day, sending croissant care packages to Jayne when she was in med school. After she'd broken their engagement, sales had plummeted.

Jayne danced her fingers over the basket, selected a croissant, then took a huge bite. 'Ooh, almond. My favourite.' She blinked a few times, then looked up at him as her cheeks pinked up. 'You remembered?'

Of course he did. He remembered a lot of things. The first time they'd gone to the cinema and she'd pretended to be scared so they could hold hands. The first time they'd kissed. The first time they'd made love. Watching her pack to go to a different university. Standing beside her at her sister's funeral.

Just about all of the big firsts that mattered in life he'd done with Jayne.

He stopped himself from reaching out and brushing some icing sugar off her cheek. Instead he said, 'I was hoping we could maybe have a do-over. Pretend the other day down at the cricket ground went a bit more...platonically. It was a bit of a shock to see you when you showed up at the surgery the next day. I—'

'Aftershocks?' she said, not unkindly.

She got it. She was feeling it, too.

Her tongue dipped out between her lips and licked away some of the sugar at the corner of her mouth. He felt a match-strike run the length of his zip.

Damn, this was harder than he'd thought.

Jayne's brows cinched closer together as she chewed on her lower lip and then, as if she'd made a decision, released it. 'Shall I put the kettle on?'

'Depends on whether or not you want to draw up a treaty.' Why was he kicking up those flames again?

Jayne bristled. 'I thought you were here to apologise.'

'I was. Am. I'm trying—'

He *was* trying. Trying not to pull his heart out of his chest and simply hand it to her, as he had all of those years ago.

He pulled his phone out of his pocket instead. This was obviously going to take longer than he'd thought.

'Go on. Put the kettle on.'

CHAPTER FIVE

JAYNE TRIED NOT to earwig too much while Sam called Greta at the surgery, but it was hard not to sit down, plop her chin in her hand and grin at him as he rattled through all sorts of complex details about his patients without a single note.

When he asked after a woman they'd both gone to school with, who'd just found out she had cancer, she went into the washroom and tried to scrub her face clean.

She scrubbed as hard as she could. The way Sam dealt with everyone he'd known since he was a boy so professionally and compassionately was…exactly what she'd expect from him. He'd been born to do this. Not literally, of course, as he was adopted, but when Mrs Crenshaw had insisted on bringing that little abandoned baby boy home there had to have been a touch of the angels about it.

She looked into the mirror to check if her face was clean. No good. Maggie's daughter had used a permanent marker for the whiskers and the nose. *Nice.*

She came back into the kitchen just as Sam was thanking Greta for saying she'd pop in on his grandad as he'd need the afternoon off after all.

Nerves bunched in her belly. She'd meant for them to have a chat, not spend the rest of the day together. Especially if he had work to do.

Stream's Edge Surgery was his pride and joy. He'd never been shy about wanting to follow in his grandfather's footsteps—saw it as the best way possible to show his adoptive family just how much he loved them. It wasn't a duty. Or a penance. It was love. He would do absolutely anything for them. It was one of the most appealing things about him beyond his being *him.* His loyalty.

When he saw she was not so covertly looking at him, Sam cupped his hand over his mobile's mouthpiece and explained to her that today was his catch-up day.

'Is that code for playing golf?' she joked.

Of the many things Sam Crenshaw was, a golfer was definitely not one of them. He'd be a bit like her in the kitchen. All thumbs and no taste buds.

He rolled those gorgeous green eyes of his and returned to his call.

The hammering in her heart slowed down a tiny bit. At least he was relaxed enough to roll his eyes at her lame joke. But if she was ever going to pull herself out of the past she was going to have to accept that things had changed—that Sam had changed.

Sure. He had a bit of a white-haired thing going on around the temples. But it was more than that. The fact he was here at all spoke volumes. When they'd split up he had protested. Said he didn't believe she didn't love him any more. But when she'd insisted that her calling was to become a surgeon at London's top children's hospital he'd finally stepped back. Not happily, but he understood a calling more than most.

His was to work in the surgery. To be with his family. To support the community that had nurtured him as he'd grown up. The Sam she'd known had let sleeping dogs lie for seven years. But this Sam—the one who'd weathered a divorce and the death of his mother...the one who'd proactively accepted a role as a caretaker for his community...this Sam was an adult. An adult asking her to confront their unfinished business.

One way or another, he looked determined to finish it.

Jayne tried to fight the nerves jangling round her insides as she filled the kettle, put a few of the croissants on a plate and then rearranged them about nineteen times. Having what was shaping up to be a serious conversation with Sam while she was dressed as a cat was…well, *awkward* was one way to put it.

Just as she was about to see if washing up liquid might take away some of the ink, he finished the call and pulled out a chair at the kitchen table.

'Shall we?'

Sam didn't miss the hint of nerves in Jayne's laugh as she slid the mugs of tea onto the table, pulled out a chair and sat down.

'This all seems very formal.'

'Well… I think I probably owe you more than a few croissants.'

She shook her head. 'Sam, you don't owe me anything.'

'I do. I shouldn't have tried to kiss you and I

definitely shouldn't have lied about the way it made me feel.'

'Ah.' She teased a flake of croissant away from the edge of the plate with her finger, then steered it round the wooden table top. 'So, what are you saying?'

He took in a deep breath. This moment had been seven years in the making. 'I'm saying it's time we each moved on.'

'What?' She looked shocked. 'You want me to leave?'

'No. Of course not. Bad choice of words. Maggie is counting on you. I just mean…there's obviously some unresolved—' He sought for a word that would capture the myriad of emotions he felt on seeing her. He settled on, 'Unresolved history. We've got to find a way to let go of the past. Move forward.'

His phone pinged, and as he was the only doctor on call he apologised and glanced at the screen.

'Anything serious?'

Sam gave her a knowing grin. 'Depends upon how having lunch with my sisters sits with you.'

Her eyebrows shot up. 'Really? They want to talk? With me?' She gave him a sidelong look. 'How do they even know you're here?'

'Greta.'

Jayne's eyebrows lifted. *Of course.* The Whitticombe Grapevine herself.

She shook her head. 'I don't know. I saw Kate the other day and I didn't really get the impression she wanted to talk to me.'

'Of course she does. Listen.' He read out the text. '"Would Jayne fancy a girlie lunch sometime? Maggie welcome. K xx".' He turned the phone towards her. 'There's even a smiley face. No daggers.'

Jayne's shoulders stiffened. Fair enough. Kate had already confessed to him that she might have accidentally-on-purpose brought up the dating thing at the cricket ground. Protective older sister. He loved her for it, but he was a grown man now. Just knowing his family were behind him in good times and in bad was all the backing he needed.

'Jay—it's not for an inquisition. They haven't seen you properly in ages and they want to hear everything that's been going on in your life.'

Precisely what he was trying to do. She'd said she wanted to become a certain type of woman…but he'd never really sat down with her and found out if those dreams she'd been pursuing so doggedly had actually come true.

After he'd reluctantly taken the ring back he'd closed the door on her every bit as much as she had on him. He could see that now.

'So…what do *you* want, Sam? From me?'

Mostly he wanted the past not to have twisted up his present so much. He wanted to be happily married. To be going to the school play and watching his own children be starfish or trees or King George III. He wanted to be *living* his life, not ricocheting between the past and present every time Jayne came to town. Had he wanted the woman he did all that with to be Jayne? Of course he had. A long time ago.

All of which meant… 'We need to find a way to become friends.'

She sucked her cheeks in sharp and fast. From her tight wince as she took a sip of tea he was guessing she'd bitten the inside of her cheek. Her go-to reaction when she was stressed.

'You all right?'

'Yup. Good. I'm…'

He watched as her eyes searched his face for something more. Eventually her shoulders dropped down and back, as if she were opening up her heart to him.

'I'm sorry, Sam.'

His own heart was rammed tight and fast in

his throat. This wasn't an ordinary apology. 'For what?'

'Everything.' She put her hands up before he could say anything. 'I mean it. You're one of the kindest, bravest, most generous men I've ever known. The last thing I ever wanted to do was hurt you, but...'

Sam gave a rueful laugh. She *had* hurt him. Hurt him more than anyone else had. As much as he'd like to say his failed marriage had cut him to pieces, Jayne's departure had hurt him far more.

'That's a rather large apology.'

She blew some air up at a few stray hairs to get them out of her eyes. 'I've made a rather large hash of things. I...' Her mouth stayed open, the words she was trying to say never finding purchase.

Sam took a croissant, teased apart a flaky layer from the rolled pastry, then put it back on his plate. 'Is everything all right back in London?'

Jags of pain darkened her eyes. 'I had a surgery go wrong at the hospital.'

His eyebrows lowered together. Now they were getting somewhere. He'd *known* this wasn't just a holiday lark.

'What kind of surgery was it?'
'Heart transplant.'

Jayne wasn't surprised to see Sam's eyebrows shoot up towards his hairline. He wasn't to know she'd finally reached her goal.

Reached her goal and failed, more like.

It isn't a failure. Sometimes things just go wrong.

Sam pushed his plate away and said, 'Impressive. You took the lead?'

She nodded. 'First time.' She went on before he could leap to any conclusions. 'As you know I've been training in paediatric cardiology.' She looked away from Sam as she continued. 'I wanted to add transplants to my skill base, so I did the general surgical rotations, paediatric training, acute medicine, neonatal paediatrics—'

When she paused to take a breath, Sam continued for her. 'Six months in transplant, hepatobiliary, cardiovascular collapse, cyanosis...'

There was more. A lot more. And he rattled through it all. Not the usual syllabus for a GP. Not that she'd thought he'd spent his time in med school learning only basic diagnostic skills then called it quits, or anything, but...

'Samuel Crenshaw! Have you been following my career?'

He feigned a casual shrug. 'I read the medical journals. I just might occasionally read up on what's happening at your children's hospital. To keep myself up to date medically...for my patients' welfare. Obviously.'

There was a glint in his eye now. A humorous one. That fuzzy warm feeling that came from knowing someone special cared lit up her chest. *Oh, Sam.*

'So, what happened with this surgery?'

She stared at him long and hard. Sam had used to be the one person in the world she could tell anything to. The embarrassing stuff. The fun stuff. The things she wished she had or hadn't done. He never judged. Only listened. And on the occasions he gave advice it was always thoughtful. Considerate.

This was her chance to take a leap of faith that he was still that man. That he really did want them to be friends.

And just like that she opened her heart to him.

Once she started talking she couldn't stop. She told him all the details. About Stella's heart failure. About keeping her alive with an artificial heart for months. The opportunity to finally do a transplant. The offer for her to take the lead.

'So…did something actually go wrong? Or do the parents want someone to blame?'

Typical Sam. Able to cut through to the quick of the matter like a hot knife through butter.

'No. The parents aren't why I took the break.'

They'd been amazing, actually. Had actually thanked her for giving Stella those precious few five months, as harrowing as they'd been.

She took another leap. 'Mind if I just unload everything on you?'

'Absolutely,' he said. 'That's what friends are for, right?'

If hearts could crumple and expand in the space of a millisecond her heart did just that. Above and beyond any romance they had shared, they had always been friends. And that was what she'd missed the most in those dark months after Jules' death.

His lips, his body, his lovemaking… Oh, they all ranked up there in Things She Missed Most in the World, but it was this…being able to just sit and talk and make sense of something with someone she could trust…that she missed more than anything.

So why can't you trust him with what you know about Jules?

She kicked the thought back into her Cupboard of Dark Things and focused in on the surgery.

'Is there something that makes you think you might have made a mistake?' he asked.

Reluctantly, she nodded.

The gesture visibly caught Sam by surprise.

She scrambled to right it. 'No. Not technically. It was textbook. But as a surgeon… Yeah. Absolutely. I messed up.'

He looked perplexed. 'How?'

'One of the junior surgeons told me where the donor heart was from.'

'Isn't that protocol?'

'Yes, but he told me the back story. The whole entire back story.' She hoped her voice carried enough weight that he would be able to figure it out on his own.

He spun his finger round. *Keep on talking*, that gesture said. He wanted to hear it from the horse's mouth.

'It was a young woman's heart. A woman who'd been riding her bicycle out on a country lane and been hit by a car.'

He let out a low whistle. 'Hell, Jay. It's a co-incidence, but…'

He was saying it was out there. But not impossible.

'But of all the surgeons in the entire world… that heart ended up in *my* hands.'

Didn't he see? The fact that it had affected her so much meant she might not be equipped to do it again. There would be more hearts. Perhaps more from girls who hadn't looked right and left before they careered into oncoming traffic.

'Did Stella die in surgery?'

It was strange hearing Stella's name coming from Sam. It felt…*intimate*. The first thing she'd shared with him since she'd left Whitticombe all those years ago.

Jayne shook her head. 'The surgery went perfectly. She died two days later. Rejection.'

Sam pushed back from the table as if the matter was settled. 'So—a straight-up rejection. There isn't anything you could've done about that. It's not nice, but it happens.'

'It shouldn't have happened to *me*. Not with *that* girl! Not with *that* heart.' The tears she'd been holding at bay for days began to flow.

Sam had her in his arms before she knew what was happening. It felt unbelievably perfect to be there. To let someone comfort her. She was so used to pushing people away. So used to pushing Sam away.

She cried and cried, accepted tissue after tissue, eventually laying her heart against his chest until the sound of her sobs abated and all she could hear was the steady thump-thump of his heart.

'Hey, you two!' Maggie appeared in the doorway.

They pulled apart as abruptly as if they'd been caught naked. Maggie's eyes glinted mischievously. She loved a bit of gossip.

Totally unfazed, she popped a finger on her chin and said, 'Oops. I'm not interrupting anything, am I?'

They both shouted, 'No!'

Maggie clicked her tongue. 'I'm obviously interrupting *something*. What's going on?'

Jayne had no idea what to say. She was supposed to be looking after Maggie, not morphing into a blubbering emotional wreck who sobbed her heart out into her ex-fiancé's shirt.

Sam swept a few stray locks of Jayne's hair behind her ear, then turned to Maggie. 'I think our Jayne, here, might need as much looking after as you do.'

* * *

Sam was just about to shoulder his messenger style bag when a knock sounded at his front door, quickly followed by a, *'Yoo-hoo... Sam-u-el?'* that could only belong to his older sister Kate.

He walked out into the hallway with his coffee cup, only to find his sister already inside, as ever 'casually' inspecting the place. A finger across the oak beam framing the inglenook fireplace... A quick tidy of a stack of medical journals beside the deep-cushioned sofa. A wrinkled nose.

'Are you still drinking that horrid coffee in the morning?'

He laughed. 'If by "horrid" you mean the Vietnamese beans I would sell my left arm for, yes. Yes, I am.'

'Sammy, that stuff will—'

'Keep me awake all day,' he finished for her.

That caught her attention. 'Haven't you been sleeping? I told you—you should get someone in to help you at the surgery.'

'It's not a problem. I love my job. Double the work means double the joy.'

His sister made a noise suggesting that she didn't believe him. No surprise there, then. It was a common trait amongst his sisters. Why believe their little brother when they could go with feminine intuition instead? Mind you, his gut was telling him a few things he was trying to ignore as well, so perhaps she had a point.

'Grandad is going to be in his cast for another five weeks, Sam. Maybe longer if he keeps insisting on bashing open doors with it.' She looked him straight in the eye in only the way a sister could. 'Be honest. How's the clinic?'

'Great,' he lied.

It was busy. And about to get more so. It was the beginning of hay fever season, tourist season, sports day season, and there would be the inevitable injuries that came with long jumps, high jumps and potato sack races. Not to mention the usual extensive list of coughs, checkups, aches, unusual bumps, infant earaches… Maybe his sister had a point.

'A little birdie tells me you've been popping over to see Maggie after surgery.'

And by 'Maggie' he knew she meant Jayne.

'Yup.' He stuffed a stack of papers into his bag, trying to give his sister the hint that he really did have to get going. 'Maggie's got a pretty serious condition.'

'I get it that you like doing the whole country

doctor thing with house calls, Sam, but Maggie has an actual *surgeon* living under her roof who just might be on top of all that—am I right?'

'Yeah, well… She's—'

His sister did one of those *Oh, don't bother lying* flicks of her eyes.

Fine. He went there because of Jayne as well. How could he not? What had come through loud and clear the other day was the fact that she was still dealing with her sister's death as if it had happened yesterday. The part of him he'd thought would never leap to her rescue again turned out not to have got the message.

Talking to her, holding her, laughing with her and Maggie over cups of tea and a board game after work… For the first time in he didn't know how long he had felt one hundred per cent whole. And if he was being really honest it felt as if he was getting a second chance.

Not with the romance side of things—he didn't even know what to do with the chemistry buzzing between them—but something deeper was at work. Something he felt they'd never had a chance to deal with all those years ago.

'You aren't trying to do your knight in shining armour act again, are you?'

'What act?' He bridled. Sometimes sisters didn't know when to leave well enough alone.

'Oh, come on, Sam.' She pointed at one of the and sat down on the other.

Here we go. Another Big Sister Talk. As much as he loved her, she was properly off base.

'Sam.'

'Kate.'

'You know as well as the entire village does that the whole reason you got together with Marie was to rescue her.'

'What on earth are you talking about?'

'Oh, come on. She was great. I'm not saying otherwise. But…'

Sam rolled his eyes. *Here it comes.*

'She had a horrible ex-boyfriend. Moved out of the city to escape him. Came to Whitti-combe to start over. You had the perfect life all sketched out, with this house, your work at the surgery… All you were missing was a woman to do it with.'

'You make me sound like a real arse.'

'Don't be silly. We know you loved her. We also know you've never really got over Jayne.'

Oh, for heaven's sake! No wonder Jayne had looked nervous about the 'girlie' lunch. Just one sister was enough to drive him round the bend, let alone all of them at once.

'Jayne and I are ancient history.'

Kate pursed her lips at him. 'You know I do not usually swear. But that is total *crap*, Samuel Crenshaw. We loved Marie. Every bit as much as you did. But the two of you… It was never the same as it was with you and Jayne. You're the only one who didn't see it.'

'Oh, c'mon, Kate. I think I'm a bit better than that.'

'Look… No one blames you for wanting to be someone's hero after what you'd been through with Jayne. You tried everything you could to help her.'

'Thanks for the reminder. I think you'll also remember that she told me to go and live my dreams because she wanted to live hers. Alone.'

He'd tried talking to her. She'd hardly responded. He'd told her he was there to listen. She'd said there wasn't anything to say. For the first couple of months she'd practically been a zombie, so it had been a shock when she'd announced she was heading back to her studies as per normal.

And on the handful of trips she'd taken back to Whitticombe since only a fool would have failed to notice she had become a different person from the one he'd fallen in love with.

Kate sighed and gave his hand a squeeze. 'After Jules died she was a lost soul. She had no idea *what* she wanted. You knew *exactly* what you wanted. And at that age it's hard to take your eye off the prize.'

He was taken aback. 'Are you saying I chose my life here over Jayne?'

'Not at all. I'm saying you were a young man. A young man who'd set his heart on living the life the two of you had always dreamed of. For Jayne that life didn't exist any more. *Couldn't* exist any more.'

She had a point. When Jayne's sister had been killed she'd been completely shell-shocked. He'd had no idea how to help someone enduring that level of grief. He'd never called a time of death at his training hospital, let alone seen someone he loved pass away.

If Jayne had clung to that pain of course it would have been traumatising for her to perform a transplant with a heart that had come from a woman who'd had a similar accident. There had been something else, though. When she'd spoken about Stella's death he'd seen something in her eyes that had looked...

haunted. As if by pursuing paediatric surgery she'd believed she could put a stop to all bicycle accidents. Or…more to the point…feel she was bringing her sister back each time she fixed a child's heart.

'Why are you frowning?' his sister asked.

'I'm not frowning.' He was. He was totally frowning. He pulled her into a bear hug and acquiesced, 'Maybe you've given me a bit of food for thought.'

'You know I'm right, don't you?'

He parted his lips, poised to protest, and instantly knew there was no point. Kate had been the one who'd driven him to complete his medical degree all those years ago, with the ring box burning a hole in the corner of his duffel bag. He still had it. Hadn't thought it right to propose to another woman with Jayne's ring, just as…

Oh, God. Kate was right. He had tried to make Marie's dreams come true with his own vision of the future. The future he'd planned with Jayne. He looked round the big open house. Marie had often said she'd felt as if there was a ghost living in the renovated barn, and he'd always told her she was being silly, but honestly… Maybe she'd been right.

That ghost was Jayne.

She'd been the one who'd stared at the derelict yellow brick building and said, 'That would make a nice place to live one day.' She'd been right. It was great. Vaulted ceilings. Thick oak beams. Windows two metres high that saw the sun rise in the master bedroom and set in the open-plan family area.

Family.

'Who made *you* so smart?' he asked.

'Mum and Dad,' she said, giving his hand a pat. 'And a splash of sisterly intuition.'

He rolled his eyes at her.

'Sammy…' His sister stretched across the kitchen island and began picking at a bowl of grapes. 'You be careful.'

'What? With Jayne? She's fine. We're just friends.'

He wondered if she could see his nose growing. Technically they weren't anything else… but there was that *thing* that hummed between them.

'Okay,' she said, suddenly changing tack. 'If things are so chummy between the pair of you, why don't you ask her to help you at the clinic. We all heard her offer. She's probably desperate to put a bandage on someone or look down someone's throat.'

Sam scoffed. 'I don't really think it's her kind of thing.'

'Why not? She's a doctor, isn't she?'

'Obviously. But she—' He checked himself.

It wasn't Jayne's surgical career that was the problem. It was the idea of having her a metre or so down that corridor where they'd planned to work together. It would be like playing at something he could never have, and in all honesty he was still at the baby steps phase of this supposed friendship.

His sister gave him another one of those X-ray vision looks of hers, then said, 'Why don't you let her decide? You're big kids now.' She patted his head in the way only a big sister could. 'If you really are friends she'll want to lend a hand. If you're not…you'll see the back of her by the end of the day.'

She briskly wiped her hands back and forth, as if she'd sorted out yet another one of the vast problems of the universe.

'Have her do a children's clinic or something. Go on,' his sister said, popping another grape into her mouth, a mischievous glint to her eye. 'I dare you.'

When Sam got to the surgery and saw the patient list bursting at the seams he knew his sister was right. He needed help. And it was just a few doors down the lane. Maybe it was time to take a chance.

CHAPTER SIX

'YOU'LL BE FINE.'

Sam handed Jayne a cup of strong coffee. Thick and black with a couple of lumps of sugar, just the way she liked it.

'And you're absolutely sure you're cool with this?'

Jayne's nerves were pinging all over the place. Not about seeing patients, but about doing it here. At Stream's Edge Surgery. They might as well unfurl a banner that said *Jayne's Back in Town! Why not get your blood pressure checked and give her a quiz while you're at it?*

Or maybe that was just her nerves at work.

'Greta's going to send all the paediatric appointments your way, but since your training did cover all the basics you'll be completely fine to handle anything else too.'

She pulled a face. 'I don't know anyone as well as you.'

He shrugged. 'Sometimes that's a good thing.

People often hide the whole truth if they know you well.'

All the air left her lungs and she looked away. Did he know she'd kept something from him all these years?

He took a long drink of his coffee, then smiled. 'I know you two are friends, but maybe a bit of distance explains why Maggie wanted you to look after her and not me. She's loving those foot-rubs you're giving her, by the way.'

Jayne disguised her relief that he wasn't referring to something darker with an airy wave of the hand. Foot-rubs were the least she could do for her friend, who seemed to run the village singlehandedly from her armchair. She'd do more if required. Much more.

If she'd been able to reach in and fix her sister's heart that day she would have, but...

She shook the image away. *Work.* Work was good. Especially with the anniversary of Jules's death coming up.

Sam escorted her to his grandad's examination room. The walls were covered with family photos and scads of hand-drawn thank-you cards. And in pride of place, on the centre of his desk, a huge family portrait with all the Crenshaws, their spouses, their children...

Looking at it made her realise just how much she'd missed by staying away.

'I'm going to be right next door. If you need me call or knock or—'

'Oh! Can we have a secret knock?'

Sam laughed. He was obviously a bit nervous, too, so adding a bit of playfulness to the day might take off a bit of edge.

'Sure. Let's have a secret knock.'

She knocked on the wall.

'Sounds like tachycardia.' He grinned.

'You knew I was doing a heartbeat?'

He shrugged. Of course he knew. He'd known everything about her once upon a time.

'Okay…how about this?' She did it again, but with the slow, steady cadence of his heart that had steadied her when she'd had her little meltdown the other day.

'That's good.'

He stuck out a hand and she gave it a solid shake.

'Good luck, Doctor. Enjoy.'

He dropped her a wink, then headed into his office.

The wink! It was *their* wink! Just the confidence boost she needed.

Before she could think about it any further,

she picked up the phone and buzzed Greta. 'I'm ready for the first patient.'

Two minutes later a little pixie-haired girl called Poppy was giving full vent to the fact that she had a slightly ingrown toenail.

'Mummy says I can't wear my favourite shoes to the concert!' she wailed.

Poppy's mother gave her a weary smile. She was around Jayne's age, but hadn't grown up in Whitticombe.

'How long has this been bothering you, poppet?' Jayne asked.

'It's *Poppy*,' the little girl said grumpily, crossing her arms over her chest.

'She's been like this for the last couple of days,' her mother explained. 'In a mood… So I suspect her toe's been hurting more than she's let on. And…well…it does look rather swollen.'

'It *doesn't* hurt. I just want to wear my fancy sandals!' Poppy insisted.

Jayne pulled a small set of steps over to the exam table. 'Why don't you pop up on here and tell me all about the concert?' Distractions always helped when children were in pain. Focusing on an injury could often make them more distressed. 'What instrument do you play?'

'My voice,' Poppy said proudly, and then

began to sing a catalogue of show tunes as Jayne eased off her shoe and looked at the very swollen toe. The nail was slightly ingrown, but not so badly she'd need to see a podiatrist. Unless she insisted upon wearing her favourite shoes non-stop.

After Poppy had finished a remarkably skilful rendition of a song from *Matilda*, Jayne applauded. 'That was great. Now... Here's the good news. You don't need an operation or to see a podiatrist.'

Her mother heaved a visible sigh of relief.

'What you *do* need to do, however, is give this toe a bit of extra TLC.'

She wrote down a list of recommended treatments, talking through it as she did so, making sure her mother and Poppy understood. Kids were always smarter than a lot of adults gave them credit for, so it was best to include them in the conversation if at all possible.

Poppy pulled a face. 'You want me to put apple cider vinegar on my toe?'

'No need to pour it straight on the toe. If you give it a soak in warm soapy water, or warm water with apple cider vinegar, it will help draw out the infection.' She went on to explain that she would prescribe an antibiotic cream and that, despite Poppy's desire to have a few practice runs in her closed-toe shoes, she'd probably be better off in flip-flops or something similar for the next week or so.

'And if it gets worse?' asked her mum.

'Come back in and we'll get you referred to a podiatrist. And let us know if she gets a fever. Then she'll need a proper course of oral antibiotics.'

The pair thanked her, and after that small triumph the rest of the day whooshed by. A bloodied nose from a scooter accident. A deep cut that required a few stitches. A little boy who was presenting with some pretty serious allergies… She referred *him* to a specialist unit at the nearby hospital.

By the time the lunch hour rocked round she was feeling as though that little bit of her that had shut down the day Stella had died was starting to spring some green shoots.

'Someone looks pleased with themselves.'

Jayne reached out to take Sam's empty coffee cup from him as she was already washing hers in the small kitchen at the back of the surgery. The building was an old house so it was a proper kitchen, with room for a table that had clearly seen its share of hastily eaten lunches.

Sam reached into the refrigerator and pulled out a plastic container with a rice dish in it. He caught her looking and held it out. 'Paella. My sister brought it by this morning. Want some?'

'No, I was going to head back to Maggie's and make her some lunch.'

'Ooh…' Sam sing-songed. 'So she's given you access to the kitchen, has she?'

'Hey!' Jayne protested feebly. 'My cooking's not that bad.' There was no malice in Sam's laugh so she conceded. 'I told her I'd pop by the teashop. Dolly is making some bespoke sandwiches.'

'I'm surprised Maggie hasn't installed secret cameras in the teashop.'

'Are you kidding me?' Jayne joked. 'If she could, she'd have them over the whole village. The more pregnant she gets, the crankier she is about everyone's follow-through. My inability to cook tops the list. I think we've eaten our way through every healthy café and takeaway in the village.'

Sam laughed good-naturedly. 'How about I come over one night and cook?'

A rush of warmth flooded through her as their eyes met. A wink and then an offer to cook? Was this *flirting*?

'Maggie would like that. And the children.'

'And you?'

It should have been a leading question. In some ways it was. For her, anyway. More proximity to Sam meant more chances that she'd fall right back in love with him and—

Wait. What?

She pulled her eyes away and began scrubbing the mugs a second time around. Of course there was a part of her that would always *love* Sam. And there had been some serious sizzle when they'd nearly kissed at the cricket clubhouse. But...*in* love? No. She couldn't do that. There were too many demons and too much guilt swirling away in her soul to plonk on a man whose heart she'd already broken once.

'I could make my roast chicken.'

That got her attention. 'The one with garlic?'

'The one with tons of garlic.'

She couldn't say no to that. She put on her best doctor voice. 'It'd be extra good for Maggie's pre-eclampsia, wouldn't it?'

There were a list of other benefits for pregnant women in garlic. Garlic boosted baby weight, reduced mum's cholesterol, helped prevent cancer and shielded them both from infections or colds.

Sam took the mugs and began to dry them, to save them from yet another sousing. 'I wasn't suggesting it because of its medicinal properties, Jayne.'

Their eyes caught and meshed as they both had the same memory. A glitter rush of sensation washed through her chest and her heart did another one of those insane dance moves inside her ribcage.

Sam had made it for her the night they had first made love. His parents had been out of town. He'd been living in a little annexe flat above their garage. His sisters had all been out on dates. She and Sam been eighteen years old and on the brink of heading off to different unis.

After giggling about kissing someone who'd had so much garlic, they'd both grown very serious. They'd promised they'd stay true to one another despite the distance. It was the night they had begun openly planning for a proper future together, here in Whitticombe.

A bittersweet memory if ever there was one.

'That'd be really nice, Sam,' she heard herself say.

He looked as shocked as she felt. 'Oh! Great. Well…see you back here for the afternoon rush, then I'll go shopping and meet you back at Maggie's.'

'Perfect.' She gave him a smile and slipped out through the back door towards the towpath that led to Maggie's cottage.

Maybe this was how forgiveness began. Revisiting old history and offering it a fresh layer to weave into the fabric that made up their shared past. Baby steps.

Her pace picked up at the thought. If she was able to make peace with her past, and all the people she'd hurt along the way, maybe then she could build some balance into her life. Balance she'd so obviously lacked the day she'd called Stella's time of death.

Patients weren't stand-ins for her sister. They were individuals needing her utmost respect and care. Not the emotional fallout from a loss she'd experienced so long ago. Look at Sam. When she'd come back to town he might easily have refused to be as open and kind as he had been. He was rising above what had happened between them and was truly making an effort to start afresh.

With that thought in mind, she vowed to start saying yes a bit more. To Sam. To the friendships she'd let fade. To life. Even if it was scary. Even if it meant testing the limits of her heart.

Sam looked out of the window and smiled. He was one of the only people he knew who liked a good summer rainstorm. Not so much because of the rain, but because of what came next. The rich flush of growth that came after it.

Or…maybe he was smiling because he had a date with Jayne tonight.

He checked himself. Definitely *not* a date. And it was also with Maggie, Connor and Cailey.

He gave his freshly shaved jaw a scrub as he ran through the details of his final patient of the day before calling her in.

He'd shaved. *Was it a date?*

The conversation he'd had with his sister poured ice on that thought. The last thing he should be doing was putting a romantic spin on time spent with Jayne. He had offered a fresh start for *friendship*. So he should play by the rules. But just one day of working together had teased away years of tension.

Medicine had always been a shared love of theirs. As teens they'd used to do odd jobs for his grandfather and the now long-retired doctor who'd used to work with him. They would fill up all the supplies. Restock cotton buds. Bandages. Make sure all the white rolls of sanitary paper for the exam beds were replenished. Simple jobs that had made them feel important.

A knock sounded on his door.

'Sam? It's Jayne. I think you'd better come quick. Greta's calling an ambulance.'

Jayne's tight tone had him up and out of his chair in a flash. Three long-legged strides and he'd caught up to her as she jogged back towards the waiting room.

'What is it?'

'Mrs Maynard from the greengrocers. It looks like she's having a stroke.'

His heart sank. Mrs Maynard had been to him a couple of times over the past few months, complaining of symptoms that sounded a lot like TIAs. Transient ischaemic attacks weren't as bad as a stroke, but they were indicators that a stroke might be lurking on the horizon. He'd referred her to the hospital, but perhaps she'd been stuck in a backlog of appointments.

The second he saw her being propped up in a chair by her niece, Deanna, he knew Jayne was right.

F-A-S-T pinged into his head. Face. Arms. Speech. Time.

From the confused expression, and the odd way Mrs Maynard was holding her body, Jayne was right to have asked Greta to call an ambulance.

He gave a reassuring smile to Deanna and knelt in front of Mrs Maynard. 'Mrs Maynard? How are you feeling?'

She tried to answer but her words were slurred, and one side of her face was now visibly drooping.

Deanna spoke at a rate of knots. 'We were coming in for her regular blood pressure appointment and to check on her diabetes when she started acting a bit funny. Said she felt a bit nauseous. Then she stumbled as if she was having a dizzy attack. Luckily we were only a few steps away, and by the time we got to the waiting room…' Deanna made a helpless gesture. 'Is she going to be all right?'

Sam's gut instinct was to assure her that everything was going to be fine, but strokes were peculiar territory. Some were minor and others put people in comas. Or worse.

'It looks like she might be having a stroke. It's difficult to tell how serious it is, but help is on the way.' He refocused his gaze on Mrs Maynard. 'Try as best you can to answer my questions. No stress. No pressure.'

She gave a half-nod and then her hand slipped off her lap as if it was a dead weight, indicating possible paralysis.

'Can you smile for me, Mrs Maynard?'

She did so, and the droop that was apparent in her face became even more pronounced.

'How about putting your hands out in front of you on an even plane? Can you do that?'

She lifted one arm, but the one that had slid off her lap remained where it was. A hint of panic entered her eyes.

Sam gave her shoulder a gentle rub. Poor woman. Blood-flow to part of her brain was being cut off or reduced, and ensuring she didn't go into panic mode was essential.

Jayne appeared by his side. 'Here's some aspirin and some water.'

'Brilliant—thanks.' Aspirin within the first forty-eight hours of a stroke always helped. 'Do you think you can take this without being unwell?'

Mrs Maynard nodded her head and with a bit of help was able to take the pill.

He took her blood pressure, which was high,

but not off the charts. Her blood sugar level was a bit on the low side. Not so good. What she really needed was a CT scan, to determine if there was any active bleeding in her brain. And if there was she'd need medication. And fast. Within three hours of the stroke was the recommended timeline.

About ten minutes later they heard the sound of approaching sirens, and shortly afterwards the paramedics were loading her on to a wheeled gurney.

Sam took the lead in rattling through the patient's symptoms and the handful of stats they had to hand. What she needed was a neurologist and an emergency centre. When Deanna explained she needed to collect her children from school Sam volunteered to go along with Mrs Maynard to the hospital.

'I'll sort out Maggie's children—get them something to eat—then come and pick you up.'

Jayne was standing just outside the ambulance. She looked in complete control. A woman who dealt with high-pressure situations on a daily basis. The kind of doctor you'd want treating you when the ground seemed to be slipping out from beneath your feet.

'That'd be great. Tell Deanna I'll text with updates.'

She nodded and smiled. The hum of connection felt magnetic, and even as the doors of the ambulance closed between them Sam knew he'd been right when he'd thought of their dinner together as a date.

Because everything he did with Jayne Sinclair involved his heart.

How he dealt with it was going to be another story.

Having been informed that Mrs Maynard had only suffered a minor stroke, Jayne arrived at the hospital a few hours later—and her jaw literally dropped at the sight of the cottage hospital's lush surroundings.

The facility had been built since she'd lived in the area and she'd not yet visited it.

To call it a cottage hospital wasn't entirely fair. According to the website she'd searched to get the address, the recently refurbished facilities might look old-fashioned, but inside the three traditional Georgian buildings they housed all the bells and whistles a doctor could dream of.

This particular building was the critical care

unit. Another housed a maternity and paediatrics unit. The third offered cancer and hospice care. The place where she imagined Sam's mum would've received care in the end.

She squished away the feelings that came with that. The fact that she hadn't been brave enough to come back and say goodbye, to thank her for all the love and support she'd given her through the years, had always been a thorn in her side.

She sighed and thought of the long list of regrets that festered away in her Dark Place. Being outside London was actually giving her the emotional breathing room she needed to look at her life with a clearer perspective. She appreciated there was nothing she could do to change the past, but maybe she could start making steps to change her future...

She parked the car and strode inside.

Sam was leaning against a central reception desk, speaking with a couple of doctors in blue scrubs. They were laughing at something he'd said. She enjoyed seeing him this way. At ease. Not with that little hitch in his shoulders he pretended didn't exist when she entered the room.

He turned at the sound of the doors opening and smiled. It was the first genuinely relaxed, peaceful smile she'd had from him in years, and it filled up her heart with squishy, gooey good things.

He said something else to the doctors, then waved goodbye.

'Friends of yours?' she asked.

He nodded. 'Sort of. In this neck of the woods we all get to know each other one way or another.'

She scanned the brightly lit waiting room, complete with a children's play area filled with soft toys. There were the obligatory rooms off to each side, where loved ones often received the worst sort of news. She'd sat in a room like that with Stella's family. She'd sat in a room like that when the emergency doctors had asked her parents if Jules was an organ donor.

Though she tried to turn away, she knew Sam had seen the inevitable sheen of the tears she couldn't seem to keep at bay these days glossing her eyes.

Much to her surprise, he put his arm round her shoulder and gave her a gentle squeeze. His hugs were like a cosy duvet on a winter's day. Perfect.

'You did well today. Calling the ambulance. Seeing the signs immediately. I'm just sorry that we're going to have to take a rain-check on that garlic chicken. I never got the chance to go and buy the ingredients.'

'Well… It was standard protocol.' She turned her fingers into pistols and did a quick draw. 'You gotta act *fast*!'

They both laughed, and Sam's hand dropped from her shoulders, then rested briefly on the small of her back as they left the waiting area and went out into the warm summer evening air. The rain had disappeared as quickly as it had arrived.

Jayne was still missing the warmth of his touch when he suddenly spread his arms wide and inhaled deeply.

'Don't you just love it?'

'What exactly are we loving?'

His eyes met hers and his smile softened. And just like that it appeared. That look she'd thought she'd never see again.

Butterflies took flight in her belly. Did this mean Sam was feeling what she was? The inevitable draw of attraction coupled with a deep, mutual respect?

'The summer, of course,' he said, his eyes still glued to hers. 'Don't you love it?'

'Yes,' she whispered. 'Very much.'

CHAPTER SEVEN

MAGGIE LET OUT a roar of frustration. 'If I sterilise the washing up gloves, could you reach in and pull these babies out?'

'Is that what you would advise *me* to do if I'd had a cake in the oven for only three-quarters of the baking time?' Jayne replied evenly.

When her friend made a *'gah!'* noise, pushed herself up and stomped off into the garden, to languish on a cushioned bench in the shade, Jayne knew that the baking analogy had had the desired effect. Leave well enough alone!

As Jayne stuffed yet another load of laundry into the washing machine, and caught a glimpse of a brightly coloured canal boat loaded with happy holidaymakers drifting past outside on the river, she had to admit she couldn't blame her for feeling so frustrated.

The weather was lovely. Everyone was out and about. Maggie would normally be scurrying around the village, organising about a zillion activities. Not to mention kitting out the seating area outside her tearoom with bunting and her annual display of sunflowers. Just last night Maggie had sobbed for a good two hours about the shop's impending demise.

'Balderdash!' her business partner—the rather fabulous Dolly Johnson—had cried when she'd come round with a basket of butterfly-themed fairy cakes. *'It's doing better than ever.'*

Maggie had only become grumpier with that little nugget of information.

This morning it was Nate. She missed him desperately. She hadn't had a good snog in over two months and she wasn't sure she could survive any longer without a kiss from her man.

Jayne knew exactly how she felt.

Not about snogging Maggie's husband, obviously, but now that she and Sam had their 'give friendship a chance thing' going on she was really struggling to keep her body's responses in check.

Working at the surgery was brilliant, but each time their hands brushed, or their paths crossed, she had these *saucy stirrings*. The man was sparking up all sorts of engines she'd forgotten she possessed.

It was an excruciatingly frustrating reminder

of just how long it had been since she'd had sex. She'd had a couple of half-hearted flings over the course of her time in London. Maybe three. Maybe a couple of ill-advised one-night stands. But…nothing had stuck. No one seemed to have that special something.

Except Sam.

The truth was she wanted him. He was sexy. And they had sparks aplenty.

She flicked on the washing machine and stared out of the window towards the surgery.

Was that such a bad thing?

Yes…if you're trying to be friends.

She caught herself running her fingers across her lips, her stomach feeling all glitterball sparkly at the memory of that near-kiss. It was like being a teenager all over again. Giggling and swooning and…her eyes flicked to the calendar…*two more days.*

All the fizz in her tummy flattened. Two more days and it would be seven years since her sister had died.

Busywork. She needed busywork. It was the perfect time to lay out the surprise she'd been working on for Maggie. Since she couldn't really go far, Jayne had thought she'd bring a project to her.

A while later she had her friend blindfolded and was leading her up the steps.

Maggie burst into laughter when Jayne finally allowed her to take the blindfold off. 'What did you do? Buy the entire craft store?'

'Pretty much. I also popped in on Mum and Dad's. The McTavishes let me have a little dig around the art studio for some watercolours *and...*' She masked how weird that had felt, being in the studio without them, by pulling something out of a drawer with a flourish. 'Their trusty glue gun.'

Maggie looked shocked. 'They didn't take it to Scotland?'

Jayne laughed. Her parents weren't really glue gun artists.

'Have you called them yet?'

Jayne sheepishly shook her head. She would. Maybe on the anniversary? Maybe after.

'So. Operation Artwork. What do you think?'

Jayne and Maggie surveyed the kitchen together. There wasn't a single surface that was visible. Glitter. Sequins. Canvasses. Piles of cloth. Reams of coloured paper. Scissors. Paints. She'd gone absolutely mad.

'I thought we could get a head start on that Homemade Art Fair of yours.'

Maggie's eyes sparkled with delight. 'Quick—I've got an idea for the glue gun.' Maggie wiggled her fingers at Jayne, then abruptly pressed her hands to her belly.

'Cramp?'

'Mmm… Nothing serious, I don't think.'

'Any bleeding today?'

'Nothing beyond the usual.'

Maggie had been spotting every now and again, which wasn't unusual. And there had been a bit of amniotic fluid. But at thirty-two weeks the more symptoms she was presenting, the greater the likelihood of the babies coming out before their due date. It wasn't insanely early, but the longer the little ones could stay put, the better.

After the cramping had passed, Jayne handed her the glue gun. A few minutes of concentrated silence later Maggie held up an abstract of buttons and glitter glue. 'What do you think? Would your parents be able to pass it off as one of theirs?'

'Ha! You know as well as I do my parents are into landscapes and sculpture.' And into leaving town at this time of year. A time full of memories.

As difficult as it was for Jayne to admit, easing back into life in Whitticombe was the tiniest bit easier without them here. Every time she looked at them she saw the loss in their eyes. Loss *she* had to own, all because of a silly desire to relive a childhood game.

If only she'd waited to tell Jules her happy news until she'd been back in London. And then what? Dealt with the wrath of her sister for keeping the happiest day of her life a secret? That hadn't been an option either. Jules and Jayne had shared everything.

Which was why becoming a paediatric surgeon had been a no-brainer. Not that it had eased relations with her parents. If anything, they had become even more distant.

Maggie and Sam's parents had all but adopted her in the weeks following Jules's death. At that point she was still meant to be becoming family, and they'd treated her as one of their own.

She'd done her absolute best always to smile, never to cry. It hadn't elicited sympathy from her own parents, so why she had thought it would work with anyone else… And yet when she'd cried about Stella in front of Maggie and Sam a few days ago he hadn't thought her weak.

She realised now that it took *strength* to open up in that way. It took power to be the honest version of herself in front of people who mattered. Well…mostly honest.

Perhaps this was the beginning of that journey. Step by step. Day by day. Could she finally allow herself to grieve? To believe in the possibility of forgiveness one day?

As if on cue, Sam rapped on the frame of the half-open barn-style door. She became swiftly and vividly aware that she was wearing only a string-strapped summer dress. As he propped his arms on the bottom half of the door and locked eyes with her goose pimples skittered up her arms.

'Mmm…smells like…'

Jayne rolled her eyes. 'I know. I know. Burnt toast. We all know I'm not winning a cooking contest any time soon. Thanks to you lot, I'm beginning to realise just how much I relied on my local deli to stave off malnourishment.'

'You don't cook at all?'

Jayne shrugged. 'I'm hardly ever home. And with every cuisine of the world on offer…no contest. Takeaway every time!'

He and Maggie both looked at her as if she was mad. They were right, of course. Her private life was pitiable. If anything, her flat was a near replica of how Jules had left it. Empty fridge. A couple of tins of date-expired tomato soup in the very bare cupboard. Two plates, two cups, two forks—and that was only because Jules had once had her over. They'd had a takeaway.

Why settle in, Jules had asked, *when all I want is to be out there?* She'd pointed out to the sparkling lights of central London with the same glimmer in her eye Jayne knew she'd had herself when she'd thought of moving into the Old Barn with Sam one day.

No wonder she hadn't learned how to cook. She was living in Jules's flat. Trying to live Jules's life. The only thing she'd managed to make her own was her job—and look how well *that* had turned out.

Maggie unsuccessfully tried to press herself up and off the chaise longue Jayne had dragged into the kitchen so Maggie could direct in comfort.

'I'm off on a walk.'

'What? I thought you wanted to make art!'

Jayne and Sam rushed over to her. Sam started taking Maggie's pulse, none-too-subtly, and Jayne knelt to help Maggie slide her very swollen feet into the only pair of flip-flops that would accept them. Nate's.

Maggie's eyes darted between Sam and Jayne. 'No way. Not with you two fussbudgets hovering over me.'

'We're not hovering!' they said as one. Then laughed. Then sobered.

Sam gave her shoulder a squeeze. 'Mags… Are you sure you should be walking about?'

'Stop your fussing. I'm just… I'm going to go down to the teashop.' Her hands slipped under her enormous bump. 'If I don't get to boss someone around who isn't one of the two of you I'll go crazy! So help me up and let me unleash some of my pent-up crankiness on Dolly.'

'It's warm out,' Sam cautioned. 'Maybe you should carry a parasol or something.'

'This is not the nineteenth century, Sam!' Maggie pursed her lips. 'The only fan I want is Nate, and I can't have him.' Her forehead crinkled and her lower lip stuck out, just as her daughter's did when Maggie insisted she finish her vegetables.

Sam and Jayne exchanged a look behind Maggie's back. Nate's absence was really beginning to stress Maggie out. And the higher her stress levels the more danger she was in.

'Don't be too bossy,' Jayne warned as Maggie waved goodbye without even turning around.

'I'm coming to get you in an hour if you don't reappear!'

Maggie slowly waddled round the corner, at which point Sam launched into a barrage of questions. How was her blood pressure? Had there been any bleeding? How were the headaches, the nausea, the swelling?

Jayne pulled out her phone and wiggled it in front of his face. 'I'm tapped in to some of the world's best obstetricians over at the London Merryweather. We've got an entire clinic of staff devoted to mothers experiencing difficult pregnancies. I've been stalking them. Making video calls. Demanding research papers. It's the only thing I do at night.'

She made the mistake of looking into his mossy green eyes. Okay. Fair enough. There was a bit of fantasising going on at night as well...but she was trying not to let that world collide with the real one.

'The point being...' she pocketed her phone '...if anything goes wrong I've got a hotline to some of the best doctors in the country.'

'London's much further away than Oxford.'

She touched Sam's arm. 'Hey... When and if Maggie needs to be in hospital she'll be in hospital. We've got weekly appointments from here on out, so I can start doing speed drills.' She crossed her heart and put her fingers up Girl Scout-style. 'I promise. I'm here for her.'

The lines of concern crinkling at the edges of his eyes smoothed out, and as they did so she saw his eyes travel round the kitchen and a smile twitch at the corners of his mouth. Underneath the extravagance of crafting materials there was a haphazard stack of children's cereal bowls, a rack of incinerated toast, and some of last night's congealed macaroni cheese. Balanced on the sink's edge was a plate of... What had that been again?

Bacon! She'd burnt the bacon, too.

Sam turned to her, with a full smile this time. 'Apart from takeaway places, doesn't London also have loads of places where you can learn how to cook?'

More flirtatiously than she'd intended, she parried, 'I've not got anyone to impress in London.'

Sam leant against the counter and shook his head. 'I don't believe that.'

She debated whether or not to be totally honest. A friend would disclose just how pants her social life was, so... *Here goes nothing.*

'I have *zero* social life.' She laughed.

She sort of did. The kind of social life that was jammed in between surgeries and forty-eight-hour shifts and trying to get a few hours of sleep. Nothing that stuck. Nothing that mattered...

'I don't believe that for a second. You're a beautiful woman. Suitors must be queuing up at your door.'

A flush hit her cheeks and Sam gave himself a silent boot in the bum. Why was he quizzing Jayne about her love-life? He wanted details of the men she'd been with just about as much as she wanted to hear him talk about his ex-wife. Not at all.

She picked up some yarn and began twirling it around her finger so tightly that the blood ran out of it.

She didn't meet his eye, but said, 'I've gone out with the odd person, but they were set-ups mostly. The type that make up a foursome when a mate doesn't want to go on a blind date on her own. It's not really my thing. Dating. Getting to where I am on the surgical side of things has been my real goal, so...'

'Snap.'

Her eyes widened with surprise. 'Seriously?

I thought you had the whole work-life balance thing covered?'

'Ha! Not so much.'

He swirled his finger in a few drops of water on the counter as his ex-wife's words echoed in his head. *'There's a ghost in this house.'*

'I think my ex would disagree with you on that one.'

He met her wide-eyed response straight on. It was the first time he'd properly mentioned his wife to Jayne. Obviously she knew about her, had seen her at Christmas, but even so…

Even so nothing. You're just friends.

'It used to drive her crazy how much time I spent at the surgery.'

'That wasn't very fair! You were just setting up!'

He smiled at the note of defensiveness in her tone.

As if she feared she'd been a bit too defensive, she playfully tacked on, 'Didn't she realise how much time it would take to steal all your grandad's patients?'

He laughed. 'All work and no play made Sam a very single boy,' he said, twisting the oft-repeated phrase to more factual effect. 'The truth is, hindsight is making it pretty clear I married her too soon.'

Once again he met Jayne's eye.

'Too soon…?' She spoke barely above a whisper.

'Too soon after you.'

Jayne's cheeks drew in swiftly as she registered what he was saying. He hadn't been over her when he'd got married. His sister was right. His ex had been right. There'd been a ghost in his house and another woman in his heart. He hadn't realised it at the time. He'd truly thought he'd moved on. But here he was, and his heart pounding against his chest was telling him what he should have known all along.

Jayne Sinclair was the love of his life.

Maybe he'd never get over her. But he sure as hell had to find a way to live with it.

Jayne scrambled to fill the awkward silence. 'Well… I obviously didn't know her…but she should've known you don't do things by halves. It's a shame she didn't stick around longer. Getting through tough times takes a while.'

Jayne stopped talking, clearly realising the words she spoke could just as easily have been about the pair of them. The words hung heavily between them.

'Has it been worth it for you?' He nudged her elbow. 'The all work and no play?'

She snorted. 'I think you know the answer to that one. The first transplant surgery I led ended with me having a bit of meltdown, so… I hate to admit it, but Sana—the nurse I told you about—she was right. I did need a break. A chance to get some perspective on things.'

She swept her tongue across her lips. Those stirrings he'd been trying to keep at bay reared up strong and vital.

She looked straight into his eyes and said, 'Sam, I—I just wanted to say… I know you and I have history…and it makes everything a bit more complicated…but I owe you a thank-you. You've been amazing since I came back. More than I deserve.'

His eyes dropped to her dress. Fresh cherries dotted across sage-green fabric. Its flimsy straps were all but begging him to reach out and just slip one off a silky-soft shoulder, then the other off the other silky-soft shoulder…

A wave of lust swept through him like wildfire. Surged past any sensible, logical lines he might have drawn in the sand. He lifted his eyes as her dark lashes fluttered against her cheeks and unapologetically she met his gaze.

The atmosphere between them shifted. The space between them hummed. Instinct took over. Before he could think better of it Sam was cupping Jayne's face in his hands, drawing her in close enough to breathe her in. Cotton. Sweet peas. Sugar.

'What is it you want from me, Jayne?'

Instead of answering she went up on tiptoe and accepted the kiss she knew he was waiting to give.

What followed was swift, carnal, and utterly satisfying. His brain barely had time to catch up with what his body was doing. Kissing. Tasting. Touching. Everything about Jayne's body language mirrored his. The same old spell that had first drawn them together unleashed itself. Nestled right back into place as if not a solitary day had passed since they'd last made love.

He wove his fingers into the hair at the base of her neck and pulled her even closer to him. His body was consumed by the need to taste her. Her lips, her tongue, that sweet spot at the base of her throat. He dropped kisses the length of her collarbone, dragged his teeth along her earlobe until he heard her moan.

The sound of her pleasure shot straight to his groin. His hands swept along her curves as he unleashed swift flicks of his tongue into that sugary nook just below her ear. The way he knew would instantly made her grind her thighs together with longing and press her hipbones into his.

Close wasn't close enough.

He wanted skin on skin.

He stepped back long enough for her to see the heat in his eyes—heat that soared in temperature as he took one of those flimsy spaghetti straps in each of his fingers and slipped them off her shoulders. He barely waited for the fabric to puddle on the floor before he was cupping her breasts, skating his hands along her stomach, feeling her shivers of response as he tugged her panties down to meet her dress.

It was insane. All of it. But it felt so good. A hot, intense reminder of just how magic the sexual chemistry between them had been. He could see it in her eyes. She hadn't forgotten it either. She wanted him every bit as much as he wanted her.

The phone rang.

'Don't answer it,' Jayne groaned.

'Not mine…' Sam growled.

She batted at the counter—presumably trying to switch the phone off—took hold of it and held it up behind his shoulder even as he swept a stack of fabric off the counter and replaced it with the two curved cheeks of Jayne's bum.

Mmm... She felt good. Each and every ounce of her.

He began unbuckling his belt as her free hand swept along the length of his erection—then abruptly stopped.

'Everything okay?' he asked against her lips, his body primed for her to fling the damn phone away so they could get back to devouring one another.

'It's the hospital. They want me to phone in.'

He could already hear her calling. And just like that the volcanic heat in him turned icy cold.

Jayne started at the sound of footsteps. She'd thought she had the small churchyard to herself, but it appeared that Monday afternoon was rush hour at the cemetery. A rush hour of two.

She looked up.

Her breath hitched in her throat.

Sam.

They'd not really talked since that super-awkward lust-fest she'd destroyed by taking that call from the hospital. It had been gut instinct.

Hospital rings. Jayne responds.

She'd tried to explain. Had insisted he would've done the same if a patient had been in need… But at the end of the day he'd left without saying anything.

Of course it was more complicated than her simply taking a phone call. Perhaps he'd come to the same conclusion she had. The phone call had been a cruel divine intervention, pointing out the obvious: they weren't meant to be together.

She'd gone into the surgery that morning, as discussed, but when her last patient had left the building she'd needed to come out here and see her sister. Offer amends. Ask for forgiveness.

'Thought I'd find you here.'

Sam's voice wrapped around her like a cashmere blanket. Soft and protective.

'Well… I figured it was safer than visiting the lane where it happened, so…'

He nodded.

She shot him a grateful smile. Despite the complication of feelings pinballing between her heart, head and gut it was comforting to have Sam here.

It was the first time she'd been in Whitti-combe on the anniversary of Jules's death. She'd thought she wanted to do it alone, but it was nice to know there were other people thinking of Jules as well.

Would her parents benefit from this? Seeing their daughter's grave and the flowers those who had also known her had left?

Jayne gave Sam a grateful smile as he nestled the potted plant he was carrying at the base of Jules's grave, then stepped back to where Jayne was kneeling and sat on the ground.

'Mind if I join you?'

She shook her head. ''Course not. The flower's lovely.'

'It's an aster. I thought it suited Jules's personality.'

'What?' Surely the aster was a symbol for patience. If there was one thing her sister hadn't been, it was patient.

'It means star,' Sam said into the silence.

She started. 'But that's—'

'Greek. I know about the patience thing, but it also stands for love of variety, and the Jules I remember loved variety.'

Despite herself, Jayne laughed. 'That was definitely Jules, all right.'

Sam's laugh blended with her own, and as their eyes met she knew he was here for all the right reasons.

He crossed his legs and leant back on his hands, his long fingers disappearing in the thick early summer grass. 'She would've liked a patient I had today.'

'Oh, yeah?' Jayne picked a dandelion and plucked at the petals.

'Definitely. An eight-year-old girl who's as devoted to her trampoline as Jules was to racing around the lanes on her bike. A real adrenaline junkie.'

Jayne tried not to sound stiff as she asked, 'Why was she in?'

'A tib-fib break after a particularly enthusiastic somersault session on the trampoline.'

Jayne sucked in a sharp breath. 'Did her parents not have one of those protective guards around the springs?'

Sam nodded. 'That and more. They had it dug into the ground so she wouldn't fall off. They had protective padding. They even had padding for her. But Carlee is her own spirit.'

'Which means…?'

Sam reached over and gave Jayne's knee a

squeeze. 'It means Carlee is probably going to be a familiar face up at Grandpont's A&E.'

'The hospital up the road?'

'One and the same.' He smiled. Not gleefully, of course, but nor was it grim.

She wondered if that was how his grandfather had thought of Jules. A live wire who, no matter how much padding she had, would have found herself at the wrong end of a poorly calculated risk at one juncture or another. Which might mean...

No. She could have stopped Jules. Laid out the rules more clearly. End of the road and *no* further.

Sam picked his own dandelion and began plucking off the petals one by one.

She loves me...she loves me not...

He abruptly ripped off the rest of the petals and sprinkled them on the grass. 'I'm sorry things got a bit hot and heavy the other day.'

'Hey. No need to apologise. It takes two to tango.'

They weren't looking at one other, but she could feel the energy buzzing between them tighten.

'I'm glad you're here,' he said eventually. 'I know there's a lot of awkwardness to sort through, but with the surgery being so busy, and Maggie needing your help, it's been a God-send.'

She tapped his foot with her flower. 'I feel like we've spoken more honestly in the past two weeks than we have in years.'

Sam laughed. 'To be fair, we haven't really talked since we split.'

True. She'd been too frightened to. Too scared to confess to Sam that she was the reason they were kneeling at the end of this grave. She should have trusted him enough to tell him. She knew that now.

After a few more moments of silence Jayne stood and stretched. 'Guess I'd better get back and check on Maggie. The kids'll be back soon, moaning about whatever gruel I manage to dish up for them.'

Sam's eyes lit up. 'Hey, want to take a look at the Old Barn on the way?'

Jayne's felt a whoosh of anticipation unfurl in her heart. 'Absolutely!'

Sam couldn't believe how nervous he was. He *knew* the house was beautiful. He and his architect father had spent years designing it. And they'd paid even more attention to detail once they'd started putting it together. The exact tiles. The precise woodcuts. The perfect window frames. He knew every inch of the place in detail.

It had been a true bone of contention with his wife.

'You love that house more than you love me!'

He'd protested. *Of course he didn't. The house was a thing...she was his wife.* He'd told her she was being ridiculous, but when she'd gone the house hadn't felt any different. Which, of course, was when he'd realised it had never really been *their* home.

As Sam and Jayne turned the corner into the cobbled barnyard Jayne's hands flew to her mouth. He watched as she soaked in all the details. The peaked roof. The dark beams standing out against the golden sandstone.

Her eyes practically glittered with delight. 'Oh, Sam...it's perfect. It's exactly how I imagined it.'

In that moment he realised just how right his ex had been. He hadn't built this house for her. He'd built it for him and Jayne.

CHAPTER EIGHT

GRETA GRINNED AS Sam whistled his way into the surgery the next morning. 'Well, would you take a look at who the lark brought in?'

'An early night and a perfect cup of coffee works wonders.'

It was the truth. After Jayne had left he'd made himself a light supper and spent the evening reading medical journals. Lately, his time at home had felt like filling a void until he could go to work again. Last night he'd really enjoyed being in the house.

He'd loved seeing it through Jayne's eyes instead of seeing it as the time-waster his ex had pronounced it to be. The poor woman. The more he thought about it, the more he wondered how they'd ever thought they were right for one another.

You wanted to be her knight in shining armour.

She'd wanted stability. Village life. A guy

with old-fashioned values. He'd given her all those things and married her with the absolute best of intentions. With love.

But in the end the love he'd had to offer her hadn't been enough. Hadn't been on the same scale as the love he'd had for Jayne.

The thought dropped a lead weight in his gut, and he was relieved when Greta handed him a full patient list. Jayne was taking Maggie to the hospital, so he wouldn't have that extra pair of hands he'd come to rely on a bit too quickly.

A few hours, a stack of paperwork and a dozen patients later, Greta rang through. 'You all right if I squeeze in an extra patient this morning?'

'Absolutely! Send him in.'

'Dr Sinclair…?'

'Ah! Mr Sedlescombe.' He got up and ushered in the elderly maths teacher. 'Come on in. Here, let me grab you a chair.'

He took one of the man's canes and held on to his elbow as his former teacher eased himself into the chair.

When Sam sat down again he did a quick scan to see if there was anything visibly wrong. A bit of dry skin on the backs of his hands… There was an aqueous cream for that. His eyes were the slightest bit watery... Nothing too out of the ordinary for an older gent.

'So, Mr Sedlescombe, what can I do for you today?'

'Well, it's a tad embarrassing.'

'Nothing to be embarrassed about here. You know as well as I do that anything you disclose to me in this room will stay right here.'

'Well...' The old gentleman, whose blue eyes still glinted brightly, leant on one of his sticks and threw a quick glance at the closed door. 'I suppose you've heard about my upcoming retirement party?'

'I certainly have. It's going to be part of the fete, isn't it?'

Mr Sedlescombe's thick silver hair caught the light as he nodded. 'Yes, that's right. They're unveiling a long-service plaque for me and the new village AED, if I'm not mistaken. A geriatric and a heart-starter. What a double bill!' Mr Sedlescombe winked.

Sam laughed. 'I'm sure it's more coincidence than a message from above.'

'That may be... But what I'm wondering about is...' He dug into his pocket and pulled out a blister pack of little blue pills.

'Oh!'

Sam's eyebrows near enough shot off his forehead. After a morning of arthritis pills, earaches and blood pressure tests, he certainly hadn't expected this. It was one of the reasons he loved his job. Constantly kept him on his toes.

'So you're interested in a bit of lovemaking after your retirement party?'

'Something like that. But the AED has got me thinking...' He pushed a newspaper clipping onto Sam's desk and tapped it. 'Says here I might have a heart attack if I take these pills.'

Sam quickly scanned the article. 'Well, this poor chap appears to have taken more than the recommended dose.' He picked up the blister pack. 'Mind if I have a look?'

A quick scan revealed they were on the level. He'd obviously ordered them through the post, but they seemed legitimate enough. Sam would be happy to prescribe some through the local pharmacy, but something wasn't sitting right... Sometimes being a GP was a bit like being a detective. A detective with particular sensitivities about people's health and emotional state. Their generational leanings... Social class...

Mr Sedlescombe had taught maths at the village school for as long as Sam could remember.

He was often in the local light opera perfor-
mances. He made a mean Christmas punch.
There were some dots he was failing to connect...

'Mr Sedlescombe. Is there something else
that's bothering you about taking these pills?'

The elderly gentleman stroked his chin, then
finally met Sam's eye. 'Please, call me Terry.
And, well... I know this isn't strictly how things
are done in the medical profession...diagnosing
by the internet and all...but the truth is I was
hoping to give them to Vera.'

'Your wife?' Vera, the retired English teacher
at the village school, had had a stroke a couple
of years back, but regular appointments indicated that everything was pretty much back to
normal. 'Why?'

'She thought they might help her.'

The penny dropped. 'Have you been looking
into clinical trials about memory loss?'

Relief flooded Terry's features. He'd clearly
been uncomfortable disguising the real reason
he'd come in.

'Okay. So, what we're really talking about
are the clinical trials that are being done on
vascular dementia?' He'd read about them too.
They were testing people in their fifties and

sixties who had had a stroke or were experiencing memory loss. 'If I remember correctly, they're about increasing blood flow by dilating blood vessels?'

Terry nodded. 'Vera ordered these things.' He picked up the packet. 'She did it in my name, so luckily I was the one who opened them up when the post came. I was hoping if you agreed with me that taking these pills is the wrong thing to do, I could dissuade her from taking them.'

'Perhaps the best thing to do would be to bring Vera down here and we can all talk about it. These aren't the pills they're using in the trials and… Well, it's still a trial.'

Terry nodded in agreement. 'I know. That's what I told her. But she won't come down. No offence to you or your grandfather, but she's taken a notion that she'd like to talk to a woman.'

There was a female GP in the next village, who came in once a week to take appointments for just such a reason, but she and her husband had decided to pack up a caravan and drive across Mongolia for the summer. Sam had been so busy he'd not had a chance to find a suitable replacement.

An idea struck. 'Do you remember Jayne Sinclair? We were in the same maths class.'

Terry's forehead crinkled as he thought back. 'Of course I do. The twin who lost her sister.' His gaze drifted to the church spire, which was visible through the window. 'Her poor parents...not quite sure how they stuck around after that.'

Sam nodded. There it was again. Disbelief that Jayne's parents had stayed in the village.

He was struck by the fact that people still remembered Jayne as 'the poor sister who survived.' What a cross to bear. No wonder she wanted to live somewhere else. The past was shackling her to the worst time in her life.

An uncomfortable feeling tightened in his gut. Was he guilty of the same thing? Had he ever really sat down and thought of her as a leading paediatric surgeon? A woman getting on with her life the best she could?

Maybe he'd been so busy reeling from rejection he'd refused to look at things from her perspective. It was obvious from her reaction to Stella's death that she took her work incredibly seriously. Stepping away from the surgical ward to ensure she only gave her patients her A-game must have taken some serious strength.

It was something he prided himself on when it came to his own patients. Being there for them with nothing less than his best. So why hadn't he been able to do the same when it came to his personal life?

The answer was as plain as the hand in front of his face.

He'd tried to fix Jayne by insisting they keep following their dreams. The engagement, the wedding, Stream's Edge Surgery, The Old Barn... He'd completely missed the fact that everything had changed for her the day her sister had died. Just as he'd missed the signs from Marie that he wasn't including her in the life he'd become so determined to live. The life he'd planned to live with Jayne.

What a pattern! Truly loving someone meant being there for them. Good times. Bad times. It didn't mean trying to jam a person into a predetermined mould. People were malleable. They changed. Love had to be every bit as flexible.

Just as Terry was trying to be with his wife as they approached old age.

He shifted in his chair and gave Terry a *We can do this* smile. 'Jayne's in town for a spell. Now, she's not a GP, but she *is* a highly respected doctor. I'm sure she would be more than happy to speak with your wife.' He glanced at his watch. Jayne should be back from the hospital by now. 'I can ring her right now, if you like. See if she'll pop in some time this afternoon?'

Another wash of relief softened his maths teacher's features. 'You'd do that for me?'

'Of course, Mr— Terry. It would be my pleasure.'

After Sam had reassured himself that everything was okay on the health front for Mr Sedlescombe, he showed the gentleman out of the office. He was completely surprised to see Vera sitting in the waiting room. Her eyes lit up when her husband appeared, bright with expectation. Terry whispered something in her ear and her eyes shot over to Sam. She gave him a brisk nod and a hint of a smile.

Crisis averted.

As he called in the next patient a familiar satisfied feeling filled his chest. *This* was why he did what he did. Now, if he could just convert that to his personal life maybe there'd be some way to see if he and Jayne could find an opportunity to give each other a second chance…

'Everything go all right at the hospital?'

Jayne nodded. 'Yup. Well, as good as can be

expected. Maggie isn't taking it quite as easy as they'd like, but the babies are still where they're supposed to be. I've tied her to an armchair and put on a reality show on extreme cake baking. I'm hoping it will hold her interest for the next hour or so.'

'Tied her to a chair?' Sam deadpanned.

'Yeah.' She shrugged. 'It's how we roll in London Town. Now, about Mrs Sedlescombe...'

She was feeling strangely nervous. She prided herself on the personal touch with her own patients, but it wasn't as if she'd learned about split infinitives from any of them. Talking to her former English teacher's wife about whether or not to take erectile dysfunction pills for memory loss felt...*intimate*. A bit like going through her granny's underwear drawer. Something you didn't really *do*.

It's something GPs do, you idiot!

She locked the thought away in the drawer marked 'Yet Another Reason to Respect Sam'.

As if he'd been reading her mind, he gave her shoulder a squeeze. She shook off the little crackles of response she felt at his touch and focused on the words coming out of his mouth. Or was she just staring at his mouth? She'd been kissing that mouth a couple of days ago. *Mmm*…it was a lovely mouth.

Wrong point of focus, woman!

'Don't worry. They know you're not a dementia specialist. Mrs Sedlescombe just thought it would be a bit easier for her to speak with a woman. I think she's more embarrassed than anything.'

Fair enough. It wasn't your everyday conversation about how to stave off the effects of aging.

'And you said Mr Sedlescombe's coming too?' She'd learned fractions from Mr Sedlescombe. And Algebra. The foundation for a lot of the science courses she'd taken in med school.

Sam threw a kind smile towards the waiting room. 'They've been married for ever. He's worried. And, as he's finally taking retirement at the end of the year, I suppose it's just another reminder that they're both getting on. He should've retired about fifteen years ago. I think Vera only retired because she had the stroke. It's sweet, really. He wants to make sure the woman by his side stays the way she is as long as she can. Even if means a bit of embarrassment at the local GP's.'

Wow. If that didn't tug at her heart strings nothing would. This was village life. In and out of each other's pockets in the best way possible.

'You lot need a female GP on staff.'

Sam shot her a look. *Whoops.* She was meant to have been that person.

'We do have a doctor who comes over from Farmstone once a week, but she's on an extended holiday. You're right, though. With Grandad getting on we probably need someone on a more permanent basis.'

She avoided his eyes just in case they were saying what her brain was… *It could've been you.*

Sam clapped his hands together, as if he was trying to dodge the awkwardness as well. 'All right. I'll call them in, shall I?'

'Sure. Fine. I'll just…' she flicked her thumb towards the office '… I'll just wait in here.'

She went into the homely room and sat down. Then stood up. Then struck what she hoped was a casual pose by the examination table.

Why was she feeling so awkward? Her patients in London were every bit as important to her. Up until a handful of weeks ago her world had all but revolved around them.

A thousand reasons played out in front of

her. They hadn't known her when she was in pigtails. Their parents hadn't driven her home from sleepovers. Not one of them had been to her sister's funeral.

She swallowed down the inevitable lump in her throat. So many of Sam's patients had been there for her family that day. Helping Mrs Sedlescombe was the least she could do.

Maybe that was how Sam felt. He could have ended up anywhere in the world. With any other family. Or in another orphanage. He knew how fortunate he'd been, and serving his community was a pleasure, not a penance.

The truth whipped in and shunted through her. Paying penance was the reason why Stella's death hurt so much. She'd put so much pressure on that one surgery to make her world right again, when the truth was nothing would bring her sister back.

As she heard Sam and the Sedlescombes walking down the corridor she made a quick vow to herself. From here on out she'd treat her patients the way Sam did. As individuals with their own journeys. Not stepping stones in her medical career. Maybe she'd never been *that* clinical with her patients, but… The truth hurt. She'd been on a mission, and that mission had failed because she'd had the wrong goal.

Once Sam had shown them in, and the couple had sat down, everything slipped into place as if she'd been having this sort of chats all her life.

Jayne showed Mrs Sedlescombe that the pills she'd bought off the internet weren't the same pills they were using in the trials. She also pointed out to Vera, as she insisted she call her, that the full results from the second stage of the trial had yet to be released.

When it became clear that Vera still had yet to be fully convinced that taking the pills would be risky, she pointed out the potential side effects that might be experienced if she took the pills she'd purchased: sudden and sharp memory loss.

The couple looked at one another in shock. And a little relief.

'I had no idea more memory loss was a side effect.' Vera looked at her husband and gave his wrinkly hand a squeeze. 'I could've made things worse if you hadn't insisted on coming in.'

'That didn't happen, though, love. Did it? We came in and Dr Sinclair set us straight.'

Vera batted at the air between them. 'I feel so silly.'

'Don't,' Jayne insisted. 'Who doesn't want to fix something that seems out of your control?' The list of things *she* wanted to fix wouldn't have fitted on a scroll that circled the earth! 'If you're genuinely worried about memory loss there are a few things I suggest for my paediatric patients.'

Terry tightened his grip on his wife's hand. 'I didn't realise children had strokes.'

Jayne sobered as she explained that anyone could have a stroke. 'The trick as regards memory loss is to keep your brain stimulated. I appreciate you both had a shock when Vera suffered her stroke, but I hope it hasn't changed how you live your life in terms of mental stimulus.'

'Well, no. I still read as much as I ever did.'

Jayne smiled as she remembered Vera's classroom. It had been filled to the brim with books. 'It was you who built her all those bookshelves, wasn't it?'

Terry smiled proudly. 'It was. I got a class who were struggling with the practical application of maths to design them. Couldn't have been prouder.'

'Right. So, that's exactly how you need to continue. Stimulate your brain. Do you play chess?'

Vera nodded. 'Sometimes we pull the board out at the pub.'

Jayne smiled. There was a stack of board games at the pub. Being social would help as well.

'Great! Keep on doing that.' She printed out a list of other exercises and habitual practices that would help. As she handed it to Vera she said, 'These are actually just wise tips for anyone who's...'

'Who's getting old and wrinkly?'

Jayne laughed. 'I wasn't planning on putting it quite like that—but, yes. As you start to get on in years, looking after yourself gets a bit trickier.'

'Well, it's a good thing I've got this one by my side,' Vera said proudly as she helped Terry up from his chair. He took both canes in one hand, linked his free arm with his wife's.

'Any more questions?'

'Only one,' Terry said, and he reached into his pocket and took out the box of pills they'd been there to discuss. 'Would you mind disposing of these? Safely,' he added with a wink. 'We wouldn't want to put the village's new AED to work any time soon, would we?'

'That we would not,' Jayne said with a smile.

She waved them off, then wandered back along the corridor. She suddenly realised a couple of her father's wildflower meadow paintings were on display there. She should call her parents. Make a better effort. Report on the news from Whitticombe for once, rather than the other way round. A sea-change from their seven-years-old habit of ignoring everything.

Sam popped his head out of his office. 'How'd it go?'

'Good! Great. They're such a lovely couple.'

Sam grabbed hold of the doorframe with one of his hands and leant out further, so he could watch as Mr Sedlescombe let his canes take his weight while he opened the door for his wife.

Jayne watched Sam watching them. He looked so happy for them. The little crinkles by his eyes were soft with affection.

'What a gentleman,' Sam said.

'You're a gentleman, too!'

'Why, Jayne Sinclair...' He made a half-bow and as he dipped low she was sure a sentimental look washed across his features. When he came back up to his full height he grinned.

'You almost sound as if you're defending my honour.'

He swept the backs of his fingers across her cheek. That crackle of electricity swept through her body in double-time as her heart did a swirly dance around her chest.

Sam's honour didn't need defending. *She* was the one who was the problem. How could she lumber someone so perfect with a girl who hadn't told her own parents about the role she'd played in her sister's death? She couldn't. And nothing would ever change that. Except, of course, taking the risk of a lifetime and coming clean.

She squeezed her eyes tight and tried to picture hell freezing over. Nope. Still bubbling and hot and awful.

'Hey, there.' Sam slid his hand along her arm and dipped his head so he could look directly into her eyes. 'What's going on? You look as though your thoughts have gone dark and broody.'

'Don't be silly.' She gave his chest a little pat, ignoring just how lovely it felt beneath her finger-pads. 'I'm fine.'

Sam stretched his arms out and pressed himself back and forth in the doorframe to his office. It was very distracting. His blond hair just about grazed the top of the frame and her eyes couldn't tear themselves away from his forearms as they went through round after round of cord and release.

The very same forearms that had lifted her up onto the kitchen counter as if she were no heavier than a cotton bud…

Before she could stop herself she lowered her voice and asked, 'Want to meet up later?'

The husky quality of her voice didn't leave any room for interpretation, and in the blink of an eye the atmosphere between them hummed with the same pent-up sexual chemistry that had launched them at one another in Maggie's kitchen.

Sam's eyes raked the length of her. He was so up close and personal he might as well have been doing it with his hands. Her skin felt tingly with anticipation of his actual touch. Blood started roaring round her body and flash flood warnings pounded in her ears.

He gave his jaw a swift scrub. 'How about I take you out instead? A good old-fashioned date? Dinner? Movie?'

She couldn't help it. She did a double-take. 'What?'

He nodded. 'Yup. We're obviously not very good at the friends-only thing, but...' He tipped his head towards the space where the Sedles-combes had just been. 'As far as relationships go, I want what they have. Always have. I wanted that with you. I thought I wanted it with Marie, but it was you all along. So... *Lord.* I can't believe I'm saying all this.'

His opened his palms wide, as if he were baring himself to her.

'I don't want to be your *I'm having a crisis* fling before you head back to London. I want more. And more starts with less. Honesty. Talking. We're human. We've made mistakes. We need to find out if they're mistakes we can forgive one another for.' He dropped her that familiar wink of his. 'So what do you say? Do you fancy a date tonight?'

She bit down on the inside of her cheek. Hard. Her body was vibrating from the bombshells Sam had been dropping all around her in a heart shape.

Commitment.

Mistakes.

Honesty.

She felt as if her insides were being ripped in two. She wanted a second chance with him.

Plain as day. But second chances wouldn't work if she didn't tell Sam about Jules.

Would he still want her if he knew the truth?

There was only one way to find out. To pull her socks right up and be brave.

The words that came out of her mouth were totally different, but she hoped he would see she was trying to say yes. Yes, she was willing to try.

'Maggie will need some help getting the children sorted with dinner and bedtime...'

Sam tipped his head back and forth, then smiled that broad, happy smile of his. 'How about we cook them dinner together? That can be the first part of our date and then I'll take you to the Golden Acorn.'

She laughed nervously. 'What? The pub in the centre of the village?'

The one where she'd tactically avoided him for the past seven Christmases?

'That's the one. Great burgers.' He grinned. His tone was still light, but there was something different about him. As if a switch had been flicked. 'We've been dancing around each other for years, Jay. I don't want to do it any more.'

The heated tingles turned cold.

'No. Don't *do* that,' he said.

'What?' She took another step back and bumped into the wall.

'Back away. It's what you always do.'

Yeah. So what? It was her thing.

Determination lit up those green eyes of his. 'I care about you, Jay. Deep in here.' He pressed a hand to his heart. 'I'm pretty sure you feel exactly the same way. But neither of us really knows each other any more. So, from here on out, if you want some of this…' he drew one of his big hands down the length of that sexy body of his '…you're going to have to come out with me. And *talk*. We've got seven years of catching up to do.'

Before she could say it was too much, too soon, too big an ultimatum, Sam ran his finger along her jawline. 'I'm not asking you to marry me. I'm asking you to do what normal people do. Date. We're not the same happy-go-lucky kids we were way back then.'

True.

'We might have changed so much we aren't a match any more.'

Oh. She would put money on the fact that wasn't true, but Sam had a point…it was a possibility.

'If the dates go well, maybe we can enjoy something a bit more…' his tongue swept across his lower lip *'…intimate.'*

Her insides went liquid. In an excruciatingly lovely way. And he still wasn't finished talking.

'And if that goes well… We carry on dating.'

'For how long?' Her voice came out breathless, even though she hadn't so much as moved a muscle.

'For as long as it takes to find out what grown-up Jayne and Sam want. From life. From each other.'

Strewth.

He wasn't saying it straight out, but she got the subtext. She needed to come clean about why she'd broken their engagement. And *then* they'd decide whether or not to continue.

'What about once Maggie's had her babies and my holiday runs out?'

Everything in her seemed cinched tight as he tipped his head back and forth.

'We'll cross that bridge when we come to it. Look. Jayne…' He pressed his hands to his chest. 'I have a life here. An adult life. With friends. My family. I'd love you to see it. Properly. This is where I want to be. Where I'm happiest. It's all well and good, us living in a little bubble while you're here, but… If you go back to the London Merryweather and decide your life is there, then we go our separate ways. For good.'

'That sounds a bit final.'

If this was what being a bundle of nerves felt like then she was a bundle of nerves. Sam, on the other hand, looked more calm, cool and collected than she'd seen him in ages. Master of his own destiny. It was powerfully attractive.

He moved the pads of his thumbs across the furrows in her brow. Smoothing them out as if he had all the time in the world.

She could barely breathe as he leant in and said, 'I need you in or out of my system, Jayne Sinclair. Ignoring you didn't work. Being mates sure as hell isn't working either. So how about we try a bit of immersion therapy? See if that does the trick?'

It was the most insane invitation she'd ever had. And completely irresistible. Saturate herself with all things Sam so that they could both officially move on…

'You'll cook up a chicken tonight for Maggie and the kids?' she asked, her cheeks pinkening at the breathlessness in her voice.

Sam's voice dropped straight down into the

heart of the *come-hither* register. 'I plan on doing more than cooking things up.'

There was no way she could say no. Not with that voice pouring through her system like hot butter.

'Okay.'

'Okay, what?'

'Let's do it. The dinner. The date. All of it.' She bit down on her lip again, trying to keep the panic from her eyes.

'You're sure? There's Maggie to consider. If this is going to send you running for the hills, forget it. It's an all-or-nothing deal.'

'Absolutely.' She bumped into the wall again, then play-punched it as if it was its fault that she'd reversed into it. She took a very definite step towards him. 'I want to go out on a date with you. *And* I will stay here for Maggie.'

The only question was…would she ever have the courage—the strength—to open up completely to Sam about the past?

'Well, then…' Sam's smile was slow in coming but worth the wait. 'It's a date.'

It was a risk. Just the sort of thing Jules would've done. Risked everything for one single perfect moment.

Like the kiss Sam was planting on her cheek at exactly this moment.

'See you at six. I'll bring the chicken.'

CHAPTER NINE

'ARE YOU DICING that shallot or trying to murder it?' Maggie called from the chaise longue.

Sam looked at the poor shallot. 'Bit of both. Doing it this way brings out the natural sweetness,' he fibbed.

He didn't know. He was still wondering what the hell had possessed him to ask Jayne to go out on dates. For the rest of the summer.

Either he was a glutton for punishment or he had actually finally hit on something. Whatever it was, he felt they were finally being open and honest with one another.

He loved her. Always had. Always would. What form that love took… Well, that was still up in the air. But it certainly felt nice to know he was finally doing something about it other than drawing invisible lines that they both kept moving.

He looked over at Jayne, who was distractedly quartering some cherry tomatoes at the table where the children were colouring. Her hair, as usual, was coming loose from the French twist she'd pulled it into. Her blue eyes kept darting up to meet his. Her lips had that extra deep red flush that came from one thing and one thing only: heightened emotions.

It was taking all his brain power not to pull the mostly cooked chicken out of the oven, pop it on the table then take Jayne by the hand and walk very, very quickly down the river lane to his house.

Just as well giving Maggie and her family salmonella was on the no-no list.

He popped the bowl of salad he'd just filled onto the table. 'Tomatoes can go in there when you're done, love.'

All the eyebrows in the room shot up at that one. He'd not called Jayne 'love' before. Judging from the streaks of red on her cheeks and the flash of her smile, she didn't mind all that much. Perhaps a bit of good old-fashioned wooing was what they needed. Courtship. Manners. Respect.

'Nice pinny, Sam,' said Cailey, Maggie's littlest.

'Do you think it matches my eyes?' Sam

tugged at the edges of the apron and struck a pose.

Maggie's children applauded. Apparently pink roses and frills suited him.

He didn't know why he was being such a show-off. Maybe to counterbalance just how quiet Jayne was being. Not in a weird way, as if she was going to bolt or anything. It was more…she was being *shy*. Though he knew that at heart a lot of her bluster and bravura was a front, he hadn't seen the shy girl he'd fallen in love with for years.

Maggie's wolf-whistle broke through his thoughts. 'Gorgeous!'

He caught her throwing Jayne a saucy wink.

'And I'm not just talking about the chicken.'

Jayne, much to his satisfaction, flushed even more deeply.

He chopped up a few bits of bacon and slung them in a small frying pan. Maggie claimed her children wouldn't eat peas. Today they would. Today he could do anything.

'Where did all the village fete artwork go? I thought you lhad a gallery's worth of artwork in progress?'

'We did.' Maggie shrugged. 'Jayne's moved everything.'

'Where?'

'To our bedrooms,' Connor said as he finished his drawing of a tree with a flourish. 'She said she didn't want you to think she always lived like a heathen.'

His eyes shot to hers. 'Oh, she did, did she?'

She licked her lips. 'As if... We just needed room at the table.'

'You normally just push everything to the side,' Cailey said, as she too wrapped up a drawing of abstract bunny rabbits.

Maggie was cackling away in the corner.

'I'm glad my cleaning attack has amused you all so deeply,' Jayne sniped imperiously.

'Oh, is *that* what we're calling it?' Maggie teased.

'Why? What would *you* call it?' Jayne asked, then immediately looked as if she regretted doing so.

'I'd call it trying to impress a boy,' Maggie said through another wave of laughter.

At which point the children began singing a song about going on a date. 'A date! A date! Jayne's going on a date! She's going on a date and the boy is *Sam*.'

Jayne dumped the tomatoes into the salad

and announced that she was going upstairs to change. 'I'll meet you at the pub.'

'What? I thought I'd walk you there, just as soon as I set supper out for this lot,' said Sam.

The children and Maggie turned to her as if they were watching a tennis match.

She shook her finger back and forth. 'No can do. If this is going to be our first proper date then I want to make an entrance.'

For the next fifteen minutes, while he pulled Maggie and the kids' meal together, he whistled.

Jayne stared at her reflection, then grabbed the make-up remover and swiped off her third attempt at casual, sexy, smoky but not too horny eyes. Maybe she should simply give her lashes a swipe of mascara and have done with it.

She closed her eyes against her reflection, trying to figure out what on earth had possessed her to go along with Sam's hare-brained scheme.

Hormones had obviously played their role, but basically she'd agreed to date him for the rest of the summer. *Madness.*

An image of Mr Sedlescombe opening the door for his wife as he teetered along on his canes popped into her head, along with Sam's voice. *'I want what they have.'*

Had she said yes because somewhere deep inside her she did too?

He'd been right about one thing. She cared for him. Deeply. More than that. She loved him. But loving him and doing right by him were two totally different things. The last thing she wanted to do was break his heart again. If she had any sort of bravery she'd rip the plaster off and tell him tonight. *She* was the reason Jules was dead. Her guilt was what had fuelled their break-up.

The only mercy had been falling in love with surgical paediatrics. She adored her job. But being back here was a vivid reminder of how she had absolutely no life beyond the hospital walls.

As strange as it was to admit, she was really enjoying being back in Whitticombe. Running all Maggie's errands. Taking the children to birthday parties and playdates. Working at the clinic...

Being here had thrown a spotlight on a side of village life she'd never experienced as an adult. Maggie was right. It was nice knowing you could actually borrow a cup of flour from your neighbour, or tap on the window of a shop that had just closed if you needed a pint of milk. People here were kind. Thoughtful. Generous.

The same people who didn't know that *she* was the reason her sister wasn't alive and well in London instead of her.

It's your life. Live it. She heard the words as if Jules herself had said them.

Fault lines had begun to appear in the narrative she'd been telling herself for years. Though she'd been through it a thousand million times, was there even the slightest chance that Jules would have slowed down even if Jayne had been able to catch up with her? Jules had always been a daredevil. She had always thrown caution to the wind. She'd never played it safe.

It's your life, that voice in her head said again. *Live it.*

'What do you mean you're *off the market*?' Ethel was looking at Sam as if he'd just grown an extra pair of ears. And feathers.

'I mean, thank you, Ethel for offering to set me up on a date, but… I think I'm okay for now.'

Ethel's eyes narrowed. He knew that look.

It was her I-might-be-your-publican-but-I-am-also-your-friend look.

'It wasn't your manners I was quizzing you about, young man. I was quizzing you about your nous. You won't be finding yourself a wife by holing up at the surgery or in that big house of yours.'

'I know. I'm not saying that's the plan.'

'Oh! So you have a *new* plan now, do you?' She pursed her lips at him and started pulling a pint. 'Are you going to let me in on this new plan of yours?'

She handed him the pint and didn't wait for an answer, which was fine. He didn't want to say. Not just yet. Ethel was about as protective as his sisters when it came to his love-life, so picking The Golden Acorn to show rather than tell everyone his plan was bordering on insanity.

He smiled and took a long draft of his pint. He was obviously infuriating Ethel, but she'd see what he was talking about in a matter of minutes. Seconds, if he was lucky.

Ethel swiped at the counter with a cloth before he put his pint down. 'What's this really about, Sam? It isn't like you to be a quitter.'

Oh, he wasn't quitting… He was—

Oh, hell.

The front door to the pub had opened and framed by a million summer roses was Jayne Sinclair.

A hush fell over the place, much the way it did in Wild West films when a woman with all the right curves in all the right places walked into a saloon in a town that hadn't seen so much as a flicker of a feminine touch in years.

Sam swallowed. Hard.

Jayne's hair was down. Flowing over her shoulders like liquid silk. Her blue eyes were clean of the make-up she often wore. Maybe a swoop of mascara. Nothing on her lips. She didn't need it.

And her dress…

It was a knock-your-socks-off number.

The blue fabric matched her eyes to a T, and the nineteen-fifties style was modest…but it was making the most of her beautiful figure. The cuffed sleeves weren't so much covering her shoulders as offering a bit of a tease of the soft, creamy skin it was resting on. The bodice hugged her torso just so, before arrowing in to a slim belt where the skirt flared out from her hips.

In the driest tone he'd ever heard from Ethel,

she intoned, 'I think I understand what your plan is a bit more clearly now, Sammy boy.'

He nodded at her, still waiting for the air to return to his lungs. Jayne certainly knew how to knock a man sideways.

That shyness he'd noted earlier was still wafting round her like a brand-new perfume. He crossed over and leant in to give her a kiss on the cheek. *Mmm.* Cinnamon…and something else. Orange? Whatever it was, it *was* a new perfume, and it smelt about as delicious as she looked.

He looked at the lemons dotted all over the fabric of her dress, then back up at her.

Jayne smoothed her hands along her skirt, then said, 'I decided to make lemonade.'

Wow. There was a lot in that simple statement. He hadn't ever thought about life handing her lemons, but there was the obvious. No one would have equated her sister's death to anything *good*, but he'd always presumed she saw her sister's accident as just that. An accident. Cruel, bad luck. A tragedy.

But tonight was about fresh starts. And making lemonade. He put out his arm, just as Terry Sedlescombe would for his wife. 'May I?'

Jayne smiled and tucked her hand in the crook of his arm. 'Don't mind if I do.'

They stopped by the bar and got a glass of wine for Jayne. Ethel shot her a difficult to read look. Half smile, half don't-you-dare-mess-with-our-boy. To Jayne's credit, she smiled and complimented Ethel on how nice the pub looked—which, of course, immediately put her back in the good books. Ethel's life was this pub, and anyone who lavished it with compliments couldn't go wrong.

'I'll send someone over with a couple of menus,' she said as they picked up their drinks.

After they'd sat down and ordered Sam lifted up his glass. 'Cheers, my dear.'

'Cheers to you, Sam.'

They clinked glasses and drank.

'So,' Sam said, suddenly very keen to make good on his silent promise to court Jayne, 'tell me about yourself.'

Three hours later Jayne couldn't remember when she'd laughed so much. She'd forgotten what a good storyteller Sam was, and life in Whitticombe had given him anecdotes in spades.

She loved watching him relive the stories as

he told them. The way his green eyes lit up bright when it was a happy one...the way they darkened when it was sad.

She nearly spat out her wine when he embarked on a story about a woman who'd got her arm caught in her daughter's hamster cage, had been bitten by the hamster, then walked into the surgery with the entire thing still attached!

'She was screaming away. Swearing she'd build the hamster a little raft and set it loose on the river. Her daughter was with her, sobbing, "No, Mummy. No! Fluffy doesn't know how to swim!" Poor Greta was beside herself.'

'What did you do?'

'Washing up liquid.' He mimed easing the mother's arm out of the cage door. 'Her hamster bite was treated and her tetanus jab was boosted and the little girl carried her fluffy pet home, scolding it all the way for being so mean to her mummy. The next year it won Best In Show at the village fete pet show.'

'Hilarious.' She wiped away a couple of tears. 'We don't get too much in the way of that sort of drama at the London Merryweather. At least not in my department.'

Sam's smile dimmed. 'I suppose things are a bit more of the life-and-death variety there?'

She nodded. They are. The last thing a parent would want is for their child to be admitted to the London Merryweather because it means only one thing: it's their only hope.

'But you enjoy it, right? It's your dream?'

She took a sip of her wine to delay answering the question. The London part? Not so much. The work part? She loved it. But discovering it wasn't enough had been one hell of a knock to her blinkered quest to do a heart transplant.

Admitting as much? She wasn't quite there yet. So she did what she always did. Changed the topic.

'How's your dad getting on? You know…on his own? It must be weird, knocking around that big house on his own.'

Despite the sombre topic, Sam laughed. 'You think my sisters let him knock around the house on his own?'

Jayne didn't have to think about it that long. 'No.' She grinned.

He cleared his throat and rubbed his hands along his chair's armrest. 'When Mum died he volunteered to look after Elf. Now whenever I come to pick the dog up he looks as though I'm tearing him away from his bestie, so it's looking like I'll be in the market for a new dog soon.' He gave a little laugh. Half wistful. Half sad.

Her heart ached for him. It was easy to see how much he missed his mum. She reached across and touched his arm. 'I am so very sorry about your mother.'

'Thank you, that's kind.' His voice was gruff.

'And very, *very* overdue.' She was about to apologise for not staying for the wake, but even making it to the church service had taken a Herculean effort. Funerals and Whitticombe weren't her thing.

Sam stopped playing with his beer mat. 'Have you heard anything from your parents?'

She shook her head, almost feeling the weight of her conscience dragging her chin down to her chest.

'Are you planning on calling them?'

'Yes. Yes, I am. But it's…complicated. Once I left for London we…' Oh, God. Her voice was beginning to crack. 'We found it easier, I guess. Moving on from things in our own way.' Which begged the question… 'Why did *you* never come to London? We'd talked about it. You doing a year or so in one of the hospitals there.'

'You *know* why,' Sam said, his eyebrows

doing that little swan-dive towards the furrow between his brows. 'You told me not to. *"Don't follow me. Do your thing. We're through."'*

'Crikey.' She covered her face with her hands, then dropped them. 'I was pretty horrible to you.'

'I won't disagree with you, but it wasn't as if life was a bed of roses for you either. So long as you're happy in London, I guess it's all turned out for the best.'

She blew some air up at a few errant hairs, then blurted out the truth. 'I love the hospital. I *really* love the work. But…'

He took hold of her hands and gave them a squeeze. 'But…?'

She saw everything she'd always wanted in his eyes. Kindness. Love. Trust.

Here goes nothing.

'I don't really have a life.'

'What?'

He dropped her hands and instantly she felt the loss of his touch.

'I thought you were always out and about. Going to the clubs. Dating. Living the life.' He did a little dance move as if that would make it all true. Sparkly and delightful.

She *was* out. She was out a lot. At the hospital.

'There might've been just an itty-bitty bit of fibbing about how social I've been.' She pinched her fingers together, then squished them tight.

She'd tried to do a few of the things she'd thought Jules would love when she'd first got her job at the London Merryweather. Clubbing. Zany charity events. Skydiving… The mere thought of that last one sent shivers rippling along her arms. None of them had stuck. No matter how hard she'd tried, they'd scared her silly.

'Looks like someone should've brought a sweater.' Sam tipped his head at the goose pimples skittering all the way up to her neck.

Jayne took the comment as a chance to skip over the obvious follow-up question. *Why do you stay in London, then?*

It had used to be super-obvious.

Because Jules couldn't.

Because Jayne needed to live the life Jules never would.

But she wasn't exactly doing a stellar job of it, was she? Would Jules have settled for second-best if there had been a better fit for her somewhere else?

She looked towards Maggie's cottage. 'You're

right. It is cold. Maybe we'd better head back so I can help get the kids to bed. Give Maggie her night-time foot-rub.'

Sam pulled out Jayne's chair and held his arm in the direction of the rose-covered path that led to Maggie's.

As first dates went it had hardly been the stuff of rainbows, unicorns and floating cupids. They'd covered his ex-wife, his recently deceased mother, his widowed father and then—skirting it, but touching on it—what sounded like her not entirely happy life in London.

But, hey. They were on a date and speaking to one another. Openly and honestly. It wasn't as if he had been expecting her to tell him she was going to give notice on her job and move back for good.

Communicating this way felt healing. It was a hell of a lot better than the hollow-eyed looks he'd received when he tried to talk to her after Jules had died.

When they reached Maggie's, Jayne gave him a soft smile. 'Thanks for dinner?'

They laughed.

'That wasn't really meant to come out as a question.'

He pulled her to him and they shared what felt like their first proper 'just like the old days' hug.

Sure. There were differences. They'd both seen and experienced things that had left marks on each of their hearts. But sometimes those scars made a person stronger.

He crooked a finger and tipped up her chin so that they were looking into one another's eyes.

'As first dates go I think it was pretty good.'

Jayne huffed out a *yeah, right* laugh.

Okay, fine. It had been weird. What *wasn't* weird was this. Holding her in his arms. Feeling her thighs brush against his. Her breasts pressing lightly into his chest. Her lips just inches away from his own.

'Was it good enough to go on another one?' she whispered.

He saw it then. The vulnerability in her eyes. And everything that made him the man he was wanted to reassure her that whatever was going on between the pair of them would work out for the best. Even if neither of them knew right now what form that might take.

'Absolutely,' he said, then dipped his head to kiss her ever so softly on the lips, the nose, the forehead. 'Sweet dreams, love.'

She smiled and blew him a kiss as she climbed the steps to the door. 'And you.'

He waited until the door had closed behind her before turning to go. It was early days, but maybe now would be a good time to feel a bit of optimism.

'You're looking rather cheery today,' Maggie observed as Jayne wiped the crumbs from the unburnt breakfast toast from the table.

How could she not? That one solitary sweet kiss at Maggie's front door had given her the first night of restful dreams she'd had in years. Sure, the evening had been unusual in terms of conversation topics, but—tempting as it was to live in a happy romantic bubble—they were doing their best to address real issues. Otherwise, how on earth were they ever going to trust one another? More to the point, how was Sam ever going to trust her.

'You're humming,' Maggie said.

'I just *love* keeping a happy, tidy home,' said Jayne on a *tra-la-la*.

Maggie snorted. 'Yeah, right...' She made a show of lumbering over to the kitchen window and looked out towards the river. 'How were my little rascals when you sent them off to school this morning? Sorry I couldn't get up.'

'Rascally.' Jayne laughed. 'And don't worry about not getting up. That's why I'm here.'

They'd been great, actually. Now that they were used to having someone else get them sorted for school. She was also enjoying being called Auntie Jayne. Before, when Maggie had had them do it, it had felt false. As if everyone were putting on a show that this stranger was a part of their lives. Now she felt connected to Maggie in a much more real way. They were proper friends again. Friends who were *there* for one another.

'Right, girlie! You ready to make some more bunting for the fete?'

'Ugh. Why did I decide it needed to be hand-made?' Maggie waddled back to her chaise longue. 'Are you sure this thing can handle me?'

Jayne laughed. 'It's been handling you for the past few weeks. I don't see why it should stop now.'

Maggie flicked her thumb in the direction of the downstairs loo. 'I just stood on the scales.'

'Oh...?' Jayne kept her reaction neutral. Weight gain during pregnancy was normal. A rapid weight gain—especially with Maggie's diagnosis of pre-eclampsia—could indicate something much, much worse. 'How much was it this time?'

'About three kilos.'

'Okay…well, let's check again in a couple of hours. See if there's any change.'

It was a lot for an overnight weight gain, but nothing to get too concerned over. Not yet, anyway.

Maggie sat down and, with Jayne's help, swung her legs up on to the cushions. 'Mmm… nice. Okay.' She started issuing instructions. 'Pull that table over here. I need a the polka dotted fabric and the one with the butterflies. And the ribbons, too, please.'

After Jayne had set Maggie up with her tower of material, ribbons and a wealth of needles and thread, she sat down at the kitchen table and poured out a jar of buttons. This huge old oak table had seen a lot of action lately. Family meals, crafting, planning for the fete, Sam's roast chicken…

She wondered if she might ever share a table with Sam that would become embedded with their own memories.

It's still early days, yet.

'Throw the scissors over, would you, Jayne?'

Jayne mimed hurling them across the room, and then presented them to her as a courtier might bring a gift to a queen.

'Thanks, friend.'

Maggie's thank-you flew straight into her heart. It was one of those special thank-yous. The type that actually meant *I knew I could count on you.*

A thought spiralled round her brain, then clattered into her heart. Had she got the trust thing wrong?

Sharing the details of Stella and the surgery had been painful, but Sam hadn't judged her. Hadn't pushed her away. He'd pulled her in closer. Told her she would heal. Told her that everyone would help, that they were there for her. In good times and in bad.

Then why didn't you trust Maggie when Jules died? Your parents? Sam?

She rammed a button onto her canvas and succeeded in gluing her finger to it. Served her right.

Living with her secret had driven such a thick wedge between her and the life she now knew she wanted to live. One with balance and friends and, most importantly, love. Sam was the love of her life, and keeping this one simple truth from him made the whole idea of a fresh start a joke.

Her mother had told her to look after Jules. When her daredevil sister had insisted they do something to celebrate her engagement, pulling out their bicycles had just popped into her mind. She'd never once thought it would lead to Jules's death. She'd pictured the two of them tootling along to the pub for a celebratory glass of fizz. Not high-tailing it down the road as Jules led, shouting over her shoulder about needing to feel the wind in her hair and the rush of danger in her veins.

As button after button went down on her canvas Jayne relived the scene.

She'd tried to catch up with Jules. Her lungs had burnt with the effort. She'd pushed and pushed her pedals as hard as she'd been able to, but despite her efforts she hadn't been as fast as that sports car had.

Since that day her life had become an endless race. A relentless push to catch up with a girl who had died because of a longing to feel the wind in her hair.

Jayne fought the urge to close her eyes, knowing the scene would play itself out yet again if she did. Instead she glued button after button.

So much good had come of the last few weeks. The renewal of friendships. The gentle healing of old wounds with Sam. She didn't want to lose that. But would honesty do more good or make her biggest fear come true? That the family and friends she loved would turn their backs on her the way she'd turned her back on them so they wouldn't see her pain.

Maggie looked up from her project and saw Jayne furiously working away. 'Show me.'

Jayne held up her canvas. A dog could have done a better job. 'What do you think?'

Maggie tried her best not to smirk. And then she couldn't hold it in any more. She laughed until tears began to roll down her cheeks.

'That bad?'

Maggie's hands moved to her swollen tummy. 'Let's just say the apple didn't fall very close to the tree when it comes to artistic abilities.'

Jayne didn't take offence. She'd never been artistic. But the comment hurt. Not only was she not anything like her parents, she had failed them in the most epic way possible.

She made a vow then and there to ring them tonight. Tell them everything. Fly up and see them if need be. Maybe face to face would be better…

She started making a to-do list in her head. The children would need help if she went. Maggie would need looking after. There were Sam's sisters… They might help. And after the surgery closed perhaps Sam could make his famous roast chicken again—

'Jayne?'

Maggie was swiping away tears with one hand and holding her stomach with the other.

'Yes, honey? What's up?'

Jayne went over to her in case she needed to be handed something. When she got there the crimson stain of blood told her all she needed to know.

She didn't need art supplies. She needed an ambulance.

CHAPTER TEN

'WHEN IS THE ambulance coming?'

It was about the fifteenth time Jayne had asked since she'd rung him.

'Soon.'

Sam snuggled the quilt up to Maggie's back as Jayne held her on her side. It would be a makeshift stretcher if the paramedics couldn't get their gurney into the old-fashioned kitchen. It would also be a protection against the hard stone floor if she had a seizure.

Once they'd got the quilt in place Jayne put a cool cloth on her friend's forehead. A distraction, really.

'Mags, try not to twist and turn so much, all right? Sam needs to insert a cannula in your forearm.'

There was no hint of panic in her voice, but Sam could see fear in her eyes. Maggie's pregnancy was going rapidly, dangerously wrong.

The paramedics' arrival time might very well be a question of life or death.

'Magnesium should help with the cramping, Mags, okay?'

Jayne stopped still for a second, swept her hair away from her shoulders and cocked her head to the left. 'I think I hear the ambulance. Shall I go out and flag it down?'

'No. They know where to come. Hold Maggie's arm steady… On my count I'm going to insert the cannula. And one…two…three. Job done.'

'The cramping's getting worse!' Maggie screamed, paled, then whispered, 'The children. Don't let the children see me like this.'

Jayne shot him a grim look.

'You stay with Mags. I'll go. There's diazepam if she starts to seize or the cramps get too severe. I've already drawn a five-milligram injection.' He pointed to where he'd put it, within arm's reach, and then headed for the front door.

He'd rung the village school, but hadn't been able to get through to the head teacher before running out of the surgery and along the river to Maggie's cottage. Seeing their mother like this would be terrifying.

Jayne mouthed a quick thank-you as she

calmly and quietly continued to make Maggie as comfortable as she could.

This, he realised, was the Jayne her patients met. Serious, compassionate, and committed to seeing things through no matter what the circumstances. Her hospital had one hell of an asset in her.

He ran out onto the lane just as the children appeared with another mum. He took her to one side and quietly explained the situation. She immediately insisted on having them over at her house for the night.

When he got back to the house Jayne was taking Maggie's blood pressure again. He raised an eyebrow instead of asking the obvious. *Too high?* Her tight expression was all the answer he needed.

Hypertension was the last thing Maggie needed. She was already on tablets for high blood pressure. They had obviously stopped working. The consequences were almost impossible to take on board. Stroke, heart failure, aneurysm...and the list went on.

'I'm not going to lose my babies, am I?' Maggie's voice was breathy and the words came out in individual gasps.

Sam knew as well as Jayne did that she could

absolutely lose the twins. They could even lose Maggie.

'I think it might be H-E-L-L-P Syndrome,' he said in a low voice.

'What's that?' Maggie wailed.

Not low enough.

He and Jayne shared a sharp look. Simply put, it wasn't anything she wanted to have.

'It can complicate a pregnancy,' Jayne said as she used a fresh cool cloth to wipe away a sheen of sweat from Maggie's forehead.

She was putting it mildly. H-E-L-L-P was a life-threatening pregnancy complication. It struck hard and fast. If she didn't get to a hospital soon the outcome was grim.

Sam had been so jacked up after that sweet, simple kiss with Jayne last night he hadn't been able to sleep. So he'd read medical journals instead. Fate, or luck, or whatever it was had led him to articles about pre-eclampsia and its equally nasty cousin H-E-L-L-P.

Sam forced himself to slow his thoughts down, focus in on the details.

H-E-L-L-P. Haemolysis. Elevated liver enzyme levels. Low platelet levels. Maggie's red blood cells would be breaking down. Her liver enzymes would be damaging the cells in her liver, leading to organ failure. All this while her platelet count would be plummeting, leading to internal bleeding. The long and the short of it meant that her life and the babies' lives were at serious risk.

Sweat was running off of Maggie's forehead as fast as Jayne could wipe it away. Her breathing was becoming tighter—a sign that fluid was filling her lungs.

'It's only a guess, honeybun. We need to get to the hospital before we know all the facts.' Jayne was soothing. She caught Sam's eye and he saw the doctor in her take over. 'She's been gaining weight over the past week. All fluid, from the look of things. It shifts when she rolls on to her side. She's also been complaining of a bit of tingling in her hands. I thought it might be because she was doing too much. Miss Arts-and-Crafts, here, doesn't *do* idle.'

'You're not blaming the *bunting*, are you? We *need* it! The village needs it!' Maggie gasped.

'No, love. Don't worry about that now.'

He nodded at Jayne. He understood what she was saying. Getting Maggie to rest properly was as easy as getting a puppy not to wag its tail.

Then Jayne delivered the punchline. 'Right

before I called you she started complaining of shoulder pain and blurred vision. Then the cramping hit, big time.'

Classic H-E-L-L-P. Although it was a difficult syndrome to diagnose. Especially without blood and urine tests.

They did the best they could to make Maggie comfortable as the wail of sirens drew closer. Sam shot outside and ran the paramedics through the scenario as they jogged towards the house, flanking a wheeled stretcher.

They entered the kitchen just as Jayne was giving a very pale-faced Maggie a cervical examination.

She looked directly at Sam. 'We need to get her into Theatre ASAP. Otherwise we're having twins right here.'

Together they swiftly shifted Maggie to the trolley and fitted her with an oxygen mask. Sam ran through the symptoms again, and then medications they'd need to counterbalance premature labour as they hurried Maggie into the ambulance.

When it was time for one of them to jump in with her Jayne deferred to Sam. 'You're her doctor.'

'No.' He shook his head. 'You're her *friend*.'

She squeezed his hand tight and hopped in alongside her.

Just as they were about to close the doors Jayne stopped them. 'Are you coming too?'

His heart slammed against his ribcage. She didn't need him there, but in those blue eyes of hers he could see it as plain as the hand in front of his face. She *wanted* him with her.

She didn't need to ask him twice.

He drove his own car behind the ambulance and ran from the car park to catch up with them as they hurried Maggie straight into an operating theatre.

When Jayne moved to follow the surgical team, one of the surgeons held his hand out as they shifted Maggie on to the surgical trolley. 'I'm sorry. We've got this now. Friends and family have to wait outside.'

One of the nurses called out. 'Blood pressure's rising. Two-ten over one hundred!'

All the blood drained from Jayne's face. *Maggie could die.*

The surgeon put his hand out again as she lunged towards the open doors of the operating theatre. 'Sorry. We need you to leave. *Now.*'

Sam wrapped his arms around her from behind and held her tight. The surgeon was right.

She was too close. Far too close. Although he could feel the fight in her, he also sensed acceptance. And if she was going to have to wait with anyone, fight with anyone, grieve with anyone, she could do it with him.

And that was one hell of a sea-change from seven years ago when her sister had been killed.

All they could do was watch and wait.

Surgeons were pouring into the operating theatre. More trolleys were wheeled in, and lamps, IV stands and meds were all steered into place around Maggie.

Jayne's eyes shot to Maggie, who was being hooked up to a fresh IV line. 'Look. She's scratching at her hands.'

They all knew what that meant. Liver failure.

'Please,' she pleaded. 'Let me scrub in.'

One of the surgeons shook his head. 'You should be calling the father. He'll want to know as soon as possible.'

'We're on it.'

Sam shifted his hold on Jayne and wrapped an arm firmly round her shoulders. She was living her worst nightmare all over again. Watching someone close to her fight for her life. Maggie was his friend, too. He got it. This was terrifying. But part of surviving was knowing when to step back.

'He's right, Jayne. We should leave them to it.'

The surgeon gave him a quick nod of thanks and then disappeared behind the swinging doors.

Jayne whirled round, her expression a mix of anger and confusion. The cool, calm, collected surgeon had quite clearly left the building.

'I should be in there!'

'No.' Sam knew he was on solid ground here. 'You shouldn't. You're like family to Maggie. Why do you think she wanted you back here in Whitticombe?'

Jayne flicked her thumb towards the operating theatre. 'Uh…that's pretty obvious, isn't it?'

'Tell yourself whatever you want, Jayne. But she didn't ask you here to be her doctor.'

She shook her head. 'Of *course* she did. We all know I've barely been home over the past seven years. I hardly knew her kids before now. I've failed her. I've not been a good friend to her. To *any* of you.'

As refreshing as it was to hear her being so honest, she was really missing the point. Hadn't she yet realised that true friendship had a way of skipping over the glitches in times of trouble?

'Good? Bad? Doesn't matter now, Jayne. You're the friend she wanted with her. And you delivered. You've been here for her.'

He put his arm round her shoulders again and led her towards the waiting room. It was directly across from a handful of smaller, quieter rooms. The rooms where they delivered the news no one wanted to hear.

When they reached the chairs she shook his arm off her shoulders. 'Sorry, I just—'

She didn't sound apologetic. He got it. She was reliving bad memories. Falling back into old habits. But he wasn't about to let her dive back into that rabbit hole again. Not after the huge strides they'd made.

'I know you're hurting. That you want a chance to fix something. But this isn't work and it definitely isn't the past.' He took her face in his hands and looked her straight in the eye. 'This is *family*, Jayne. Right here and now. And family stick together. Especially when times are tough.'

He stopped her when she started to protest.

'She called you because she was scared—and having you here helped reduce that fear. You

are *not* the person who should be in there delivering those babies. You are the person who
should be out here, praying and hoping and
doing everything else a friend who loves someone does at times like these.'

It was tough love at its cruellest.

He knew she'd been in a waiting room much
like this before. Hoping. Praying. Covered in
blood just as she was now.

This was a make-or-break moment for her.
One he was going to have to stand back and
watch even if it pulled his heart straight out of
his chest.

She could either choose love, family...*him*...
and all the messy joy that came along with that,
or go back to the treadmill in London. Fixing
and fixing and fixing tiny little hearts and hoping that one day it would heal the wounds she
was so obviously still nursing.

As the seconds ticked past, and her eyes
flicked again and again to the wide surgical
doors, Sam realised that the foundations of
friendship and healing they'd built over the
summer would either come true...or she'd run
again. Run as if her life depended on it.

Jayne's lower lip had begun to quiver. She
was visibly fighting the emotion, swiping at

non-existent tears. There was a battle raging between her heart and head and he had no idea which was winning.

She blew out a shaky breath, and in the most frightened voice he'd ever heard from her asked, 'Do you think she'll be okay?'

It was an awful thing to admit, but Sam didn't know. She was asking him for moral support, not false assurances, but... By God, he would have given anything in the world to say yes.

This was one of those awful cases where medicine and nature were fighting one another. It was a race against time. For Maggie. For the babies.

It might be that there would be three coffins at a funeral.

It might be that there would be one hell of a christening party.

Only time would tell.

As they sat, silently waiting, he tried to put himself in Jayne's shoes. Imagine what it must have been like that day all those years ago, sitting and waiting, covered in bloodstains as she was now.

Though Jules had been declared brain-dead at the scene they had still brought her in. Triple-checked that there wasn't the slightest hint of neurological activity.

Jayne had sat in a chair like this. Hoping and praying. She'd seen doctors appear, fresh from the operating theatre, sombre expressions on their faces, asking her parents to come into one of those quiet rooms. She'd heard their wails. Their cries of despair. Their pain.

Something he hadn't remembered for years suddenly pinged to the fore. It was hardly the silver lining they were looking for, but he thought it was something worth remembering.

He enclosed her hand with his, rubbing the back of her palm with his thumb. She didn't try to yank it away, so even though she wasn't looking at him, he knew she was listening.

'You know, I don't know if this is any solace to you, but when I think back to Jules and you and me, and all the things that went wrong after she died, I try to remind myself of the good that came from that day.'

'What are you talking about?'

There was a coldness in her tone that scared him, but he persisted. 'The lives Jules saved.'

'Again.' She tugged her hands free and balled them into fists on her lap. 'I have no idea what you're talking about.'

'Jayne, c'mon… You remember. The organ donations.'

'What?' She looked at him as though he was telling her a story about aliens taking over the village, not recounting actual facts.

'You must remember. The only reason your sister lived as long as she did…the reason she was able to become an organ donor…was because of *you*.'

Jayne's look of disbelief had never been more complete. 'No, it wasn't. The reason she *died* was because of me.'

Now it was his turn to be confused. 'What are you talking about? You two were out riding your bikes. It wasn't your fault that sports car came by when it did.'

Jayne looked him straight in the eye and said, 'It was my fault that she was there when it did.'

'What are you *talking* about?' he repeated.

The words came tumbling out. 'She came home to celebrate our engagement. You know Jules… She couldn't do it in any ordinary way. A huge hug and a kiss weren't enough. She wanted to *do* something. So I suggested we race our bikes down to the pub. The winner had to buy the other a glass of fizz…'

Sam's stomach turned. He knew which way this was going.

'She wanted to race. I didn't. So I was dawdling. I was frustrating her. Which always made her want to go faster. She said she wanted to feel the wind in her hair so she took off her helmet. Threw it in a hedge. It took me a minute to pick it up and then I couldn't catch her. I tried so hard but I couldn't catch up.'

Sam felt his skin go clammy as the information sucked the oxygen from his lungs. Jayne held herself responsible for her sister's death. If Jules hadn't come home to celebrate their engagement...

Hell. What a load to bear.

Losing someone you loved was hard enough. But feeling *responsible* for it in the wake of what should have been the happiest time of your life... How did a person crawl out from beneath that sort of guilt?

She had to be made to see it from a new perspective. It was the only way she could allow herself to live again.

Jayne *wasn't* guilty of Jules's death. If the logic she was using applied it would mean *he* was complicit too. If he hadn't proposed...

Oh, God. Had she been trying to protect him

from owning any of the guilt by heaping it all upon herself? But if that sort of logic worked it would be never-ending. *Everyone* would end up being involved.

If they hadn't been at the same school... If her parents hadn't moved to Whitticombe... If his parents hadn't adopted him...

No. Life didn't work like that. Jules had been an adrenaline junkie and that car had been speeding.

Plain as.

There was no way he was going to let her carry this on her own any more.

'Jayne—you *created* life that day...you did not destroy it. You did CPR. Kept the blood pumping through Jules's heart. To all her organs. That was why she was able to be an organ donor. You saved at least three other lives that day.'

'It doesn't matter how many lives were saved that day!' She looked up to the ceiling, dragged her fingers through her dark hair and shook her head. '*Urgh.* I don't mean that. Of course I don't. What I mean is, I destroyed the one life that mattered to my family. To *me*.'

She may as well have stabbed him in the heart. The *one* life that had mattered?

Again, life didn't work like that. His father was a case in point. His world had completely revolved around Sam's mum...but had her death stopped him from living life? For a while. Yes. But not for ever. Grief slashed wounds into souls. But souls and hearts healed. The scars made them stronger. More resilient. Capable of a fiercer and more determined love.

Jayne had obviously never let those wounds heal.

Her blue eyes were savage with grief. A grief he was powerless to salve. Forgiving herself was the only way she could move on from this. Just as he suspected he was going to have to forgive himself for putting his heart on the line again with her.

He didn't just 'feel deeply' for her. He knew that now. He loved her. He wanted to be with her. But there was no chance of that love flourishing if she was going to prioritise her baseless guilt over their battling life's tougher moments together. So it was time for him to start asking the questions he'd been afraid to ask all those years ago.

'Is this why you gave my ring back?'

She nodded in the affirmative. 'I didn't want you to be burdened with someone who'd done something so awful. I know. I know. It wasn't fair on you. But I wasn't exactly seeing things straight, and once I got back to London…'

She sighed heavily as memories weighted her to the chair.

'I guess I stopped seeing everything from my point of view and only saw it from hers. The clubs she would never go to. The nights out she wouldn't have. The surgeries she would never complete. It reached a point where I couldn't bear knowing her dreams were going to go totally unfulfilled.'

'So that's why you stayed in London?'

She nodded. 'I know. It's horrible. And it was cruel to you because I loved you so much. But…'

Her eyes jumped to the surgical suite. A sickening feeling swept through him. The gesture spoke volumes.

Jayne had changed track on her medical studies because she had been following Jules's dream. No wonder she'd fallen to bits when Stella had rejected the donor heart. It hadn't been just a surgery gone wrong. It had been much bigger than that. She'd failed at making her sister's dreams come true.

A sour taste ripped through him. The bitter

taste of finality. Whatever happened with Maggie and the twins would make or break her. Make or break *them*.

He could walk away now. Admit defeat. Or he could hold his ground and stay true to his conviction that they belonged together. Either way, no one—not even the girl who might break his heart twice—deserved to carry that much grief around with her.

'Jay, listen.' He waited until she met his eyes. 'You are *not* to blame for Jules's death. Just as you aren't to blame for what is happening today. A speeding driver killed Jules. And that man is living with the consequences of his actions at this very moment. The last person who should be taking the blame is you. It is not your fault.'

She shook her head. 'No. You're wrong. If I hadn't called her she wouldn't even have been in Whitticombe. She'd wanted to go rock-climbing that weekend but she cancelled it.'

'Rock-climbing?'

'Yeah. If she'd gone rock-climbing instead she'd be here right now.'

Seriously?

Jayne was spiralling. Not seeing the wood for the trees. Jules had always courted danger.

As awful a thought as it was, if it hadn't been the cycling it might've been the rock climbing. Or the abseiling…or old age. They'd never know. What he *did* know was Jayne was going to have to find a way to stop blaming herself for Jules's death.

'Do your parents know you feel this way?'

Her shoulders moved up to her ears and then dropped heavily. 'We haven't ever really talked about it. They were so… I don't know…' She drew in a jagged breath. 'My mum specifically asked me to look after her. They knew she was a daredevil. They knew she needed looking after and I didn't do it.'

'Have you *asked* them if they blame you?'

Tears glazed her eyes as she shook her head. 'Let's just say actions speak louder than words.'

She didn't have to explain. Jayne's parents had never really been the touchy-feely type, and after the accident they'd kept to themselves more than ever. Even hired someone to run their art gallery so they wouldn't have to.

No wonder Jayne was afraid to speak to them.

All her life her mother had appointed her as Jules's wingman. The one person who would keep her safe. Hence the surgical career. And now even that had let her down. And little wonder. As much as Sam knew that Jayne loved medicine, the destiny she was trying to fulfil wasn't hers. How could she be truly happy if she spent the rest of her life trying to make her sister's dreams come true at the expense of her own?

But what did a man say to the girl of his dreams when all this truth came tumbling out?

He did the only thing he could think of. He reached out and held her hand.

Jayne shifted in the increasingly uncomfortable chair. It felt as if days had passed since they'd arrived at the hospital, but it had only been an hour. Maybe two. Still too long for the news they were waiting for to be good.

She tried Sam's method of hunting for a silver lining.

They were in the right place.

Nate was on his way.

Sam's dad had rung to say the base in the Middle East had put him on a helicopter to the nearest airbase and he would be back in the UK as soon as humanly possible. The Royal Air Force was pretty dependable on that front.

'Through adversity to the stars' was their motto. Through adversity to Oxford would do for today. If the heavens shone down on Maggie and her family it would show that the stars—maybe even Stella and Jules—had been playing their part, too.

She should go and get coffee. Or biscuits. Something. Make a show of thanking Sam for not bolting when she'd poured out her blackest thoughts to him. For reaching out and holding her hand when she'd needed it most.

As good as it had felt, there was still a parent-sized hole in her heart. Until she spoke to them as honestly as she'd spoken to Sam she wasn't sure she could begin the journey of grieving and forgiveness she so longed for.

'Hey…' She gently nudged Sam, who was staring blindly at a two-years-old magazine. She knew he wasn't actually reading it because he had yet to turn the page and they'd been here for two hours.

He looked up at her, his eyes impossible to read. She tried not to react. They were both going through the emotional wringer right now.

'I'm going for a walk.'

He nodded. Unsurprised. Didn't meet her eye. 'I'll call you if anyone comes out.'

She gave his shoulder a squeeze. 'Thanks.'

He flashed her a quick smile, then went back to staring at his magazine.

As she wandered the corridors no matter how hard she tried to clear her head her thoughts kept circling back to Sam. He was such a good man. When she'd poured out her story to him he hadn't recoiled. Or judged. He'd done what she had always hoped he would do, but had been too frightened to find out.

He'd soothed her. Assured her she'd done the best she could in an impossible situation. He had been awfully quiet since then, though. Something had shifted in him now that he knew the whole story. She saw it in his eyes. Felt it in the change of his demeanour.

The truth hit her hard and fast.

She'd chosen her grief over Sam. Over a *life* with Sam. Maybe it was even deeper than that. She'd chosen grief over life.

Sure. She was a top-rated surgeon because of it. She saved lives. But the one place…the one *heart* that mattered the most…she'd left behind.

Of course Sam wouldn't meet her eye. By revealing her secret—the most important secret of all—she'd shattered the fragile trust they'd been building together over the past few weeks.

He'd all but handed his heart to her on a

plate. And she hadn't reciprocated even when she knew damn well she loved him with every cell in her body. She'd been too afraid to burden him with the guilt she'd never wanted him to own.

She'd held too much too close.

Was it too late to put things back together again? Being here, waiting on a knife's edge for news of Maggie and the babies, had pulled everything into crystal-clear focus. She had to confront the truth that had been staring her in the face for years.

She couldn't live Jules's life for her. Jules was gone. Unless she lived her own life she would never be happy. And the life she wanted included Sam. It included Maggie. It included Whitticombe and all the bunting and the sunflowers and the village fetes and everything else that came with it. Namely...her parents. The two people who had taken Jules's death every bit as hard as she had.

She pulled to a halt outside the maternity unit window. That same spot she regularly found herself at in the London Merryweather when she needed to give her heart a bit of a boost.

She needed to see her parents. The things

they had to talk about were far too big for a phone call.

A list of priorities snapped out in front of her with military precision.

Be here to see Maggie and the babies come out of surgery.

Ensure Nate was by her best friend's side.

Give in her notice at the London Merryweather.

She still wanted to be a surgeon. But she also wanted a life outside of the hospital. The London Merryweather had been Jules's jewel in the crown. It didn't have to be Jayne's.

Yes. She'd do that, then get on a plane to Scotland.

Until she made her peace with her parents she would be unable to give herself completely to Sam. It was possible she wouldn't get any resolution from them, but until she tried she couldn't give her entire heart to Sam.

A baby began to wriggle in its tight swaddling, her tiny fingers peeking out from the edge of the blanket, clasping and unclasping as if searching for her mother.

She heard someone approach, but didn't turn.

'Gorgeous, aren't they?'

Sam's voice trickled down her spine just as it always did. Warm. Comforting. Loving.

She bumped her shoulder against him, knowing that if she spoke her voice would crack and she'd tell him right then and there just how much she loved him.

She needed to speak to her parents first. Then she'd tell him. Tell him every day for the rest of their lives if he was up for it.

Just then two surgeons appeared from round the corner.

Maggie's surgeons.

Her heart leapt to her throat as they approached.

They looked exhausted.

She felt Sam's hand take hold of hers. They both squeezed tight.

CHAPTER ELEVEN

BLOOD POUNDED SO LOUDLY in Jayne's ears she had to lip-read the surgeon's words.

When she saw Sam's smile near enough hit each of his ears, there was no doubt she'd heard properly.

'They all made it.'

Sam whooped as he picked up Jayne and swung her round, both of them laughing as happily as a pair of newlyweds.

Looking into his sparkling green eyes, she realised just how many times she'd imagined moments like these. Being held in his arms, being swung round with nothing but joy in their hearts. At their wedding. When they had their own babies. At the start of one of the good old fashioned lust-fests that seemed to come so easily to the two of them.

A flicker of something she couldn't identify flashed across Sam's eyes, as if he'd been thinking the same thing and then remembered they weren't a couple.

He put her down as quickly as he'd picked her up and turned his focus on the surgeons.

He was right, of course. Maggie was who was important here. Not her bag of mixed-up feelings.

She heard all the words. *Emergency Caesarean... Catheters... Epidural... Anaesthetist... High blood pressure... Cords around babies' necks... No oxygen deprivation... Mum was awake to hear them both cry.*

Jayne pressed her fingers to her mouth to stem a small sob. Sam punched the air as if he himself were the proud father.

Almost everything that could have gone wrong, had. But the things that had gone right were the ones that counted.

'The little ones are in the NICU,' the surgeon said when Jayne asked if the babies were with Maggie now.

'Boys? Girls?'

Maggie hadn't wanted to know. She had always loved a surprise.

'One of each.'

Jayne shot a look at Sam. Just as Maggie had hoped. They shared one of those smiles that helped everything slide into place. She loved this man. Loved him to within an inch of her life. Maybe more. And she wanted what he wanted. Love. Marriage. As many babies as they could handle. Holding hands when they were eighty. Fighting each other's corners.

And yet she could see the reserve in Sam's eyes. A reserve that spoke volumes.

He knew she hadn't forgiven herself, and until she did...

How could everything she dreamed of be so close and still so far away?

She forced herself to tune in to the surgeon as he updated Sam. 'The babies are a bit small, but as you know a lot of twins come early. Not all of them under this much stress, but if they're anything like their mum, they're fighters.'

Jayne shot a quick look up at Sam, then asked the question on both their minds. 'So, Maggie...? She's definitely all right?'

The list of things that might have caused permanent damage was long. Too long.

'She will be. The water weight obviously wasn't helping. She lost a lot of blood, and the C-section took a lot out of her, but the fact she made it this far is a credit to the pair of you.'

Jayne refused to take the praise. 'I think all the credit can go to Maggie on this one.'

They sobered as their thoughts turned to the many women who'd died in the same situation. The fact that the three of them were safe and sound was little short of a miracle.

The surgeon shrugged. 'Have it your way, but it sounds to me as if she had a pretty good support team.' He tipped his head towards the far end of the corridor as if the matter were settled. 'As I said, the little ones are in the NICU for the night. We want to keep an eye on them. And Mum is obviously going to need time to recover. Any word on Dad's arrival?'

Sam pulled out his phone and checked his latest text. 'Looks as though he'll be here in a few hours. By sun-up.'

One of the surgeons cracked a joke about speeding tickets and the RAF.

'They probably had to strap him into the cargo hold to keep him from the flight deck.'

They all laughed, picturing a wild-eyed Nate trying to commandeer a jet so he could get to his wife and hs new babies and hold them all in his arms.

Jayne's eyes caught and held with Sam's. He itched to wrap his arms round her and hold her again. He saw strength in her gaze. Love. Love she wasn't yet prepared to admit she felt. That was fine. He had time.

He reached out and took her hand in his.

Her breath caught and his gaze dropped to the base of her throat, where he could see her pulse pound. Oh, she could see it. all right. See the love in his eyes.

He squeezed her hand, willing the heat streaking across her cheeks to be shared passion and to make their love the real deal. Complex. Supportive. Honest.

They'd been down this road before. Sam offering her a lifetime of love. Jayne running for the hills.

Her blue eyes glistened with everything he'd seen the day he'd asked her to marry him: hope. Hope and love in equal measures.

Oblivious to this silent exchange of information, the surgeons shook hands all round, then showed them where Maggie's room was. As expected, she was sound asleep, with one of Nate's T-shirts clutched in her hand. His way of being there, Maggie had said. As long as she could smell him she could get through anything. And she had.

At Jayne's suggestion, she and Sam walked to

the NICU for a peek at the babies. They weren't allowed in, as they weren't the parents, but one of the nurses wheeled their incubator over to the window so they could see the infants. They were holding hands.

Sam reached out to take Jayne's hand in his and together, hand in hand, they walked back to Maggie's room.

'Probably time we got some sleep,' he whispered, standing at the end of Maggie's bed.

'This chair flattens out into a bed.' Jayne pointed to a large recliner by the window. She handed him the thick blanket she'd found in the room's cupboard. 'Why don't you take the first shift, seeing as you were at work all day?'

'You sure?'

'Absolutely.' She did a little jog in place. 'You know me. Always a bit restless. I'm going to call Cailey and Connor's sitter. Let them know everything's okay.'

That wasn't the full story.

'Jayne. What's going on?'

It was a loaded question and both of them knew it.

She sucked in a sharp breath, as if she were building up courage, and then said, 'I need to leave. There are a few things I need to sort in my "other" life.'

All his senses shot to high alert. 'What does that mean? Are you going back to London now your job here is done?'

'No. That's not it. Not right away, anyway.' She wouldn't meet his eyes. 'I just... I know it's hard to put your faith in me, with all we've been through, but unless I do this I... Oh, Sam.'

Pain had replaced the love he'd seen shining in her eyes.

'Please just trust in me. Believe that I'm doing what's best. For both of us.'

She gave his cheek a quick kiss. Kissed Maggie's forehead, then left the room.

Staying awake wasn't much of a problem for Sam, with a thousand new questions burning holes in his head.

It was his own damn fault. He'd let himself become immersed in a 'Whitticombe love bubble' way too early. She had a life in London. What had he expected her to do? Drop it all and come running back to him for a life of wedded bliss? She also had unresolved issues. Shaking off seven years of pent-up guilt wasn't something that happened overnight.

He shook his hands open, as if the gesture would take his dark thoughts with it.

This was life. This was love.

The only thing he could do now was pray that Jayne found the strength to forgive herself. If that didn't happen they really would need to draw a line in the sand.

As the plane came in for landing Jayne could hardly believe how beautiful it was up in the Outer Scottish Isles. Azure crystal-clear water. Sandy white beaches. If it hadn't been so chilly and a palm tree or two had been dotted round the place she would've deemed it tropical.

It was remote. Very remote. There wasn't much further north a person could travel to 'get away from it all' unless the North Pole and thermals was their thing.

A part of her hated the way she'd up and left Sam, but she'd seen the way he'd looked at her once they'd found out Maggie and the babies had made it.

He was ready. Ready to embark on the rest of his life. She wanted to be the woman who went on that journey with him, but until she'd come clean to her parents and had their forgiveness she wouldn't ever be able to forgive herself for the pain they'd all endured.

It had taken her a couple of days to build up the courage. There were other steps she needed to take to try and face her future—with Jules still in her heart, but with enough room for her to pursue her own dreams. One of those was to be back in Whitticombe.

With her heart on her sleeve, she'd gone to the London Merryweather and told them she was going to apply for a job at the paediatric unit in the hospital in Oxford. They'd been surprised, but had said they understood, and they had told her there would always be an open invitation for her in those 'extra-tricky' cases. Cases like Stella. Then they'd handed her a letter of thanks from Stella's parents that had near enough broken her heart.

She'd read it on the plane.

In it they said the only way they had survived those five awful months with their daughter in hospital was knowing that Jayne had been the one looking after her. They knew transplants came with risks. They also knew they'd had five extra months with their daughter they wouldn't have had if Jayne hadn't been her doctor.

It was a powerful letter to read on the way to see her parents. A pair of people who experienced a similar loss. Without the chance to say goodbye.

The captain was asking the stewards to prepare for landing. She took in a deep breath.

Ready or not, she was about to embark on the rest of her life. As Jayne. Living Jayne's life. No more trying to live someone else's dreams.

After leaving the small airport and walking through the small village, she hit upon a low row of stone cottages, just as her instructions from the McTavishes had detailed. She walked to the cottage at the end with bright red window frames. Flowers tumbled out of boxes, much as they did in Whitticombe. She wondered whose personal touch it might be. Mrs McTavish's or her mother's.

Only one way to find out.

She lifted her hand and knocked.

'Do you think we should put the bunting up a day early or on the morning of the fete?'

Sam stared blankly at the village's mayor and shrugged. He didn't know. The love of his life had disappeared. Again.

Okay. This time there was a proviso, but…

Back on Sunday.

Who the hell sent a text like that?

A woman who hadn't found a way to forgive herself.

'Right,' said the mayor when Sam didn't answer her question. 'Why don't we do this with a show of hands?'

Sam distractedly raised his hand as his brain tried to connect one dot to another. No matter which way he tore the message up and put it back together again, he didn't like what his brain was telling him.

History repeats itself.

'Sam? Are you voting to keep the cake stands over by the river?'

Oops. They'd moved on from bunting. 'Absolutely,' he said, a bit too jocularly. He sounded falsely cheery, and from the look on everyone's faces they'd heard it too.

'Even though the swans stole Mrs Johnson's crumble cake last year? We almost lost two Victoria sponges as well,' Dolly reminded him sternly.

Hell's bells. How could he concentrate when one measly text was all he had to work with?

Was Jayne coming back to cut her ties for

good? Or to beg him to unearth that ring he'd never quite managed to return to the jeweller's? Or none of the above?

When he'd walked into the village fete meeting today, as Maggie's proxy, questions had been lobbed at him like arrows on a battlefield. How was Maggie? The babies? Any names yet? How was Nate? Over the moon or flat-out exhausted? When were they coming back? Would they make it to the fete? Where was Jayne?

That was the one question he couldn't answer.

London was his best guess.

Realising that Jayne blamed herself for her sister's death had been a revelation. He'd had no idea. He'd also seen the weight of guilt ease… just a bit…when she'd unburdened her heart and had seen he wasn't going anywhere.

He wished he'd known years ago. A burden shared and all that…

Blaming herself for a death that wasn't her fault… Trying to live the life her sister couldn't… No wonder she'd found coming home so hard. Living a happy, contented life with her childhood beau in Whitticombe would have seemed like dancing on her sister's grave.

There was only one way out of this endless cycle of pain for Jayne. Forgiving herself. Whether or not she was capable of it... He guessed he'd find out on Sunday. Forty-eight incredibly long hours away.

In the meantime here he was, trying his damnedest to decide whether or not the three-legged race should come before or after the egg and spoon race. Or were they still on cake theft by swan?

'Sam? Do you think we could count on one of your sisters to keep tabs on the cake competition and perhaps put Jayne in charge of the three-legged race?'

Back on Sunday.

'Sam?'

He forced himself to focus on Mrs Sedlescombe as she repeated the question.

'Will Jayne be on hand for the fete?'

He didn't know. 'Maybe... She said she would be.'

She'd also once said she'd marry him.

No. That wasn't fair. Life had thrown one hell of a spanner at the pair of them. She'd gone to a far darker place than he'd thought. And he'd let her go. Hadn't fought for her as intensely as he might have. Hadn't seen the point. He'd been too young to know better. Too unequipped to deal with rejection.

He thought he'd moved on. He'd dated. Met and married a terrific woman. He had loved Marie. He truly had. But he saw now that the love he had given her had been far from complete. How could it have been when he'd been so busy pouring himself into the two things he had meant to do with Jayne? Without hearing what his wife had been telling him.

They needed their own dreams and goals. Not to try and live out someone else's.

Ha. That was rich. The same thing that had hobbled Jayne's happiness had hobbled his own.

As painful as it was to admit, his ex-wife had been a rebound. A rebound from the love of a lifetime.

The only saving grace was that he knew how happy Marie was now. Their brief shambles of a marriage had led her to her own happy ending.

Silver linings.

Unbidden, he heard Jayne's voice in his head

the night they'd had their date at the pub. *'Why didn't you come to London?'* she'd asked.

He had thought she was talking about work. But what if that hadn't been it at all? What if she'd been asking why he hadn't come after her?

He glanced at his watch. If he left now he could be in London within a couple of hours. Maybe even before she put herself back on the roster at the hospital.

She didn't belong there. Not by a long shot. She belonged here in Whitticombe. With him. He'd seen how happy she was here. How much she loved being with Maggie's children. The soft look in her eye when she pressed her nose up against the glass at the maternity unit. She wanted what he wanted. She was just scared to reach for it.

Well, who wasn't? He sure as hell was. But this time he wasn't going to let fear stand in the way of their happiness.

'Sam?'

The villagers were all giving him that sympathetic look again. The one that said they weren't quite certain about what was going on, but they were pretty sure it involved Jayne.

Right! He'd vowed once not to be the guest

of honour at a village-wide pity party and it looked as if he was going to have to do it again.

Everyone jumped as he clapped his hands together and gave them a swift rub. 'Egg and spoon first. Three-legged race after. It's always funnier. Cakes away from the river. Decision made. So.' He scanned the group. 'What's left?'

Oli Dickinson, the local butcher, pulled a rather grubby-looking piece of paper out of his pocket and slowly began to read. 'We've got yer Whack a Mole, of course…'

'That's always a winner,' chorused the committee members. None of whom could clearly imagine a village fete without one.

'Ethel's bringing over the skittles from the pub. I'm bringing the Hook a Duck.'

'Good.' Sam was barely registering anything the poor man was saying. Time was a tickin'. 'Anything else?'

Oli listed a few more things—a human fruit machine, a ring toss and a few other things Sam didn't quite catch. How could he? He was about to change his life for ever.

'Of course we're going to need one more volunteer for Dolly's stand.'

'I'll do it,' Sam said.

The sooner they wrapped this up the better. Presumably Dolly was setting up a baked goods stall selling scones and cakes from the teashop, with all of the proceeds going to the hospital looking after Maggie and the babies.

Everyone looked shocked.

'What?'

They all shared complicit glances, then smiled benignly at him.

'As long as you're happy, Sam,' Dolly said. 'I'll bring a couple of spare towels and some wet wipes.'

'What for?' he asked absently.

He gave his jaw a scrub. He supposed he could have shaved a bit more neatly. And probably worn a nicer shirt, given he was about to make a massive declaration of love, but he wasn't looking too scruffy, was he?

'You *do* realise you just volunteered to be on the cream pie stall?'

He hadn't. He pretended he had. 'Got it. What's next?'

'That's about it!'

'Great!' He had to get to London, find the girl of his dreams, get a ring on her finger and then bring her back to Whitticombe, where she belonged. 'See you on Sunday afternoon.'

* * *

Four hours in rush-hour traffic and a speeding ticket later, all Sam's hopes plummeted to the core of the earth.

Jayne had been to the hospital. Just long enough to hand in her notice.

No forwarding address. Not for a scruffy-faced man running in off the street, anyway.

It was private information, the HR secretary had said. *Family only.*

He'd wanted answers.

He'd received them.

If only they were the answers he'd wanted to hear.

CHAPTER TWELVE

JAYNE COULD HARDLY believe what she was hearing. Her parents didn't need to apologise to *her*.

It seemed they'd all gone through their own form of torture and, with the clarity hindsight always offered, she could see they'd all unnecessarily gone through the pain alone, when they could have come together as a family.

They'd lost one of the family. Who was equipped to handle that sort of devastating loss with grace and an eye on the future?

Now that they were here, together, one thing was very clear. It was time for them all to let go of the pain. It was time for them all to heal. Together. As a family.

Her mother took Jayne's hand in hers—the first time she'd done so in years. It felt warm and comforting. Tears filled her eyes as she spoke.

'We handled it so poorly. The more we withdrew, the more we saw Jules in you. That fighting spirit that carried on no matter how tough things were.'

Jayne's mum reached out to hold her husband's hand too.

'You seemed so much better equipped to take care of yourself and…to our shame…we let you. We failed you, Jayne.'

As much as the little girl in Jayne needed to hear that her parents knew they should have reacted differently, she knew now that the blame didn't lie in anyone's camp. The apology that had been lodged in her throat for the past seven years finally came out.

'You didn't let me down. If I'd spoken to you then, told you what really happened, maybe we could have gone through it together.'

Her parents looked at her sharply. 'What do you mean?' asked her father.

Her voice shook as she spoke. 'I'm the one who suggested we ride our bicycles.'

Her father paled and her mother stemmed a small sob.

Jayne forced herself to continue. 'Jules said we should go to the pub and get a celebratory glass of fizz, so I suggested we race our bikes there like we used to. She threw her helmet off so she could feel the wind in her hair. You know what she was like…'

They both nodded. There was no need to remind them how much of a daredevil Jules had been.

'I picked it up for her, but fell behind. I saw the car coming, but I didn't scream loud enough. I tried.' Her voice cracked straight down to her broken heart. 'I tried so hard. But I wasn't fast enough to help.'

At long last she wept. Wept with her parents' arms around her as they soothed and held her.

After who knew how long, they finally pulled apart.

'Jayne, darling. Have you been blaming yourself all this time?' her father asked.

'Of course. It *is* my fault. If I hadn't suggested it things might have been different.'

'It wasn't your fault,' Jayne's mother said solidly.

Her eyes were red. Her cheeks were still wet with tears. But there was a resoluteness in her Jayne hadn't seen in years.

'It was an awful, awful accident. Nothing more. You did everything you could.'

Jayne's father rubbed his wife's back and turned soft blue eyes to his daughter. 'I think what we've learned is that we turned away from each other at exactly the moment we should have turned *to* each other. You coming here has helped us see that a bit more clearly.'

'Even now that you know everything?' Jane tugged a tissue out of the box and swept away her own tears.

'It brought you to us, didn't it?'

She nodded. 'Yes... I have to admit that when I got back to Whitticombe and you weren't there, even though I knew you were here, I... I felt as though I'd driven you away.'

'What?'

Her parents looked shocked.

'That's not true at all,' her mother protested. 'We love you. And do not think for one second that we have ever blamed you. It was not your fault. We just... We found being in Whitticombe difficult. Looking down the lane every single day, tensing at the approaching roar of a car. The whole reason we loved the village was how safe it had made us feel, and without either of you girls there it...'

'It didn't feel the same,' her father finished for her. 'But maybe it was *us* that wasn't the same, rather than the other way round...'

He began to apologise again, but Jayne held

up her hands. They were beyond playing Pass The Guilt. 'I absolve us all. We're...' Her voice shook with emotion. 'We're all *human*, aren't we? There are a lot of things we could've done better. Sticking together was one of them.'

And telling Sam she loved him. She should have done that before she'd left. She could do it right now, but even sending him that paltry text had seemed wrong, somehow. Particularly when coming here had been so powerfully healing.

She offered a silent prayer that she hadn't messed things up with Sam. Hadn't ruined them for ever.

Her father tucked a stray strand of hair behind her ear, just as he had when she was a girl. 'We're so proud of you, darling. So very proud of everything you've done with your life. We just hope you live the rest of your life for *you*. Jules was a bright, beautiful star, and we were so lucky to have had her, but now we're going to have to carry her here.' He pointed at her heart.

In that instant a lifetime of distance and misunderstanding was erased. The courage to make the final change barrelled into her heart like a beautiful racehorse surging towards the finish line. Jayne knew what she wanted. She knew where she was going and what she was doing. And she knew who she wanted to do it with.

'You two up for taking a spontaneous trip to Whitticombe?'

'C'mon, old man! Show me what you've got!' Sam was doing his best to bait everyone who came along to the pie throwing stall. Even poor Martin Cainen, the butcher. One of the nicest chaps he'd ever met. And one of the vainest.

Sam knew any reference to his age would throw him off.

'Bring it on, you old wrinkly! Do your best to hit the Pie Man!'

Martin threw him an odd look. Fair enough. He wasn't exactly exuding charm. Reeling from being too late to find Jayne was more like it.

Family only.

She *was* his family. Was meant to be his *wife.* He'd even dug the ring out of his drawer and felt it searing through the fabric of his pocket straight through to his skin. Ah, well. She clearly wasn't coming back. It would be onwards and upwards from here on out.

Seeing as his face was already covered with

cream pie, he figured he could scowl all he wanted till his bad mood decided to take a hike and let him get on with it.

Back on Sunday.

They were already thirteen hours into Sunday and so far there was no sign of Jayne.

'You going to throw that pie or eat it?'

Sam made a wild face and Martin took the bait. He missed by a mile.

A new punter stepped up to the plate. A woman holding a pie in front of her face. A woman he would have known if she'd been holding an armful of pies and wearing a Victoria sponge on the top of her head.

Jayne Sinclair.

The way his heart slammed against his chest was all the confirmation he needed to know that he hadn't expected her to show.

Especially with such a big smile on her face.

A number of people fell into line alongside Jayne. Maggie. Nate. Each with a baby strapped to their chest and holding a child by the hand. His father was there. His sisters. His grandad. Jayne's mother and father.

He let out a low whistle. *That* was a surprise.

And it explained Jayne's mysterious absence. They were holding hands. Smiling. Wearing the same light glow of serenity that he'd been praying Jayne would wear one day. The luminescence of a woman at peace with herself. The warmth of forgiveness.

Her hair wasn't combed. Her clothes were wrinkled. She looked as though she'd been travelling all night. She was absolutely beautiful.

'You going to take a shot?'

'Maybe. But first I think you'd better know that I love you.'

His heart skipped that same old familiar beat. She loved him. But was it the kind of love that meant sticking around?

'Yeah? Well…what are you going to do about it?'

She grinned.

Everyone took a step in.

'Stick around for a while.'

'Uh-huh?' He needed more than 'a while' before he bit.

'For a lifetime, if you're good with that?'

'What about the London hospital? They told me you'd handed in your notice.'

Her eyes widened. 'You went to the hospital?'

'Of course I did. Let the woman of my dreams run away to the big smoke twice? Wasn't going to happen.'

A complication of emotions washed across her features. 'I should've told you. A girl should definitely *not* withhold information from her boyfriend.'

'Your boyfriend?' He was being cheeky now, but if he couldn't be cheeky with the love of his life when she was holding a cream pie in her hand and her heart in the other when could he?

'If you'll have me.'

Damn. There was a hitch in her voice.

'Of course I will, woman. You're the love of my life.'

The smile came back. 'Well, since that's the case... I thought I'd ask you a question.'

'Go on, then.'

Everyone leant in.

'How would you feel about being more than a boyfriend? Maybe...a fiancé?'

Blood shot to his brain so fast he saw stars. When he regained his focus what he saw up close and personal was Jayne. Those blue eyes of hers brimming with hope. Her cheeks all pinked up with nerves and anticipation. This was Jayne with her heart on her sleeve, in front of all the people they loved most.

Could a lifetime of happiness be as simple as saying yes? They had a past. A complicated one. But they could have a future. A beautiful, rich, fulfilling future. So long as he could trust that she would stick it out with him.

She bit down on her lower lip and then released it. 'I know I have a pretty dodgy track record, so I thought maybe this would help.'

She knelt down in front of the ridiculous wooden cut-out they had him posing in and held up a piece of paper.

'What's that?'

'It's a contract.'

'For marriage?'

He was about to tell her he hadn't really expected things to move quite that quickly when his eye caught a few of the words on the contract. It was a job offer for Jayne from the children's hospital in Oxford. Just up the road.

Was this enough? Enough to prove she would stay for good this time?

Jayne's heart was pumping so hard she could practically see it pounding through her shirt.

What she was feeling right at this very instant was what she'd been waiting for her entire life.

Hope.

Hope that her love for Sam could finally blossom. In the light. In front of everyone she loved. Everyone who mattered. Hope that they could work through their problems together, no matter how painful it might be. Hope that they would have a family of their own.

She knew change didn't happen overnight, but she was ready to try. Right here. Right now. In front of everyone who cared enough to hold her accountable to the vows she hoped she would one day make in front of them all. To love, value and cherish the love that Sam felt for her.

She stared into his face, trying to read the mix of emotions sending flashes of dark and light through those green eyes of his.

Trust was the biggest problem. She hadn't done anything over the years to win it. Quite the opposite, in fact. But she was ready and willing to do everything it took to win it back and hold it dear.

So she would tell him as much.

In as loud a voice as she could manage, she said, 'Samuel Crenshaw. I love you. I love you with all my heart. I know I haven't been the most consistent part of your life, but if there's one thing I've learned it's that honesty is the best policy, and the biggest lie I've been telling myself all these years is that I could survive without you. I was wrong. Crazy wrong. I love you. And there isn't *anything* that will stop me from loving you with all my heart for the rest of my life, if you'll have me.'

He looked at her. Blinked. Then disappeared out of sight.

Her heart plummeted to her gut. He didn't believe her. She had known it was a grand gesture that could go wrong, but she had hoped with every fibre in her being that he would say yes.

All of a sudden Jayne felt herself being lifted up off the ground. Before she had a chance to exclaim, Sam was kissing her. Kissing her right there, in front of the entire village, as if they were the only two people in the world. As her body arched to meet his kisses she finally began to understand what was happening.

He was saying yes. Sam was saying yes. He'd be her fiancé. And one day he'd be her husband. Together they would do whatever it took to stay together. Openly. Honestly. And with the loving support of their community.

And that was exactly when the pair of them began to be pelted by cream pies.

They kissed through all of them. Banana cream. Lemon meringue. Chocolate cream. Every flavour under the sun. They were a mess. They were also crazy in love.

Sam swept a blob of meringue away from Jayne's forehead. 'Fancy jumping in the river to make this engagement official?'

She felt as if a thousand roses were blooming in her heart. A jump in the river? It was the *perfect* way to make a new beginning.

'Why not?'

They clasped hands and together, as a couple, they jumped into the river, laughing and whooping. Because with love everything had a silver lining.

CHAPTER THIRTEEN

'OH, MAGGIE…IT'S PERFECT.'

Maggie beamed as she twisted another cupcake into a just-so position on the massive tower. 'Nothing less for my bestie!'

'Right. So…' Jayne's fingers moved to her throat to touch the pear-shaped necklace Maggie had worn to her own wedding. 'Thank you for the "something borrowed".'

'Absolutely. The "something new" is that amazing dress.'

They both grinned as Jayne did a twirl in the pleated, tiered maxi-dress, sending layers of white tulle fluttering.

'"Something old"?'

Jayne poked her toe out from beneath the hem of the maxi-dress. 'Mum's wedding shoes.'

Maggie gave them a round of applause.

'And "something blue"?'

Jayne held out her wrist to show off her bracelet.

'Ooh…that's pretty. Is it new?'

'No. I found it in Jules's jewellery box. We bought them together years ago but I lost mine. I thought it'd be a nice way to share my wedding day with her.'

Before she had a chance to cry, a knock sounded on the doorframe of the village hall.

Maggie squealed. 'Sam Crenshaw—don't you know it's bad luck to see the bride before your wedding?'

'There are a whole lot of things that we haven't done by the book, so why start now?'

Sam strode in, swept his hands across the white gown stretching over Jayne's curved belly and dropped a kiss on her cheek.

'You look beautiful. I've brought you a present.'

'You didn't have to do that, love. You're all the present I need.'

Maggie rolled her eyes. 'I'm going to leave you two alone. You've got that lovey-dovey look in your eyes again.'

'How could I not have when I'm minutes away from marrying the man of my dreams?' Jayne parried.

'Good point. Get on with it, you two… The pub is stuffed with well-wishers, waiting to see the happy couple make their way down the aisle.'

'Have Ethel tell them to get inside the church and we'll be there when we're good and ready!' Jayne laughed.

When Maggie had gone, Sam pulled Jayne as close as her pregnant belly would allow. 'Are you good and ready to become Mrs Crenshaw?'

Jayne pulled a face—a frown-grin. 'Hmm… I was thinking something more along the lines of Sinclair-Crenshaw.'

Sam unleashed a slow grin of his own. 'I don't care what you call yourself so long as you're going to be in the church to let me put a ring on your finger.'

Jayne answered with a soft kiss. Of course she would be. Nothing would stop her. 'So what's this present of yours, then?'

'Go on. Open it.'

Tears sprang to her eyes when she unwrapped it. It was a plaque.

'The Jules Sinclair Bicycle Trust?'

Sam nodded, his own eyes glassing over. 'I thought, as we're on our way to having little ones of our own, we could have their Auntie Jules helping them out when they're ready to start riding bicycles.'

He told her he'd already organised for the charity to offer free helmets and cycle training to all the children in Whitticombe, as well as put up new traffic awareness signs around the village.

'Oh, Sam, it's perfect.'

'I'm glad you like it.' He leant in to give her a proper kiss, then pulled back.

'What?' Jayne laughed. 'Am I so fat with Baby Crenshaw you can't kiss me any more?'

Sam shook his head. 'It's not that. When I kiss you again I want to be kissing the bride... not the bride-to-be.'

'Well, go on, then.' She shooed him out through the door towards the stone church across the green. 'I think we've both waited long enough for that kiss.'

A few minutes later, with her father on one side and her mother on the other, Jayne stood at the entrance to the church, smiling at her husband-to-be, waiting at the altar.

It had taken them a long time to get to this point. But if she'd learned anything she now knew that some risks were worth taking. Especially the risk of falling in love.

* * * * *

LET'S TALK

Romance

For exclusive extracts, competitions
and special offers, find us online:

f facebook.com/millsandboon

⊙ @millsandboonuk

🐦 @millsandboon

Or get in touch on 0844 844 1351*

For all the latest titles coming soon,
visit millsandboon.co.uk/nextmonth

*Calls cost 7p per minute plus your phone company's price per
minute access charge

Want even more
ROMANCE?

Join our bookclub today!

'Mills & Boon books, the perfect way to escape for an hour or so.'

Miss W. Dyer

'Excellent service, promptly delivered and very good subscription choices.'

Miss A. Pearson

'You get fantastic special offers and the chance to get books before they hit the shops'

Mrs V. Hall

Visit millsandbook.co.uk/Bookclub and save on brand new books.

MILLS & BOON